# New Era Publishing

## PRESENTS

# TERRORIST IN BROOKLYN

## Revolutionary or Conspirator

*Written by: Anthony Brewer*

Published by:
New Era Books
1211 Atlantic Ave, Suite 303
Brooklyn, NY 11208

ISBN: 978-0-9844071-1-8

Male Cover Model:  BRANDON FERARY

Cover designed by: HOT BOOK COVERS

Visit Website: www.newerabooks.net

Email: newerapublication@aol.com

First Print: September 2011

Made in Brooklyn

# ACKNOWLEDGEMENTS

I wrote this entire book based on the different views expressed while listening to Amy Goodman, the then and now host of the WBAI show DEMOCRACY NOW.

She educates, informs, instructs and shares information unbaisedly for her listeners to decide. Thank you Amy Goodman and Juan Gonzale

**OUR LIVES ARE CONTROLLED BY INFORMATION AND HOW WE APPLY THAT INFORMATION.**

There is only one God regardless the name we call out in our times of need.

It does not matter your color, race, culture, style, religion or philosophy, that is yours and you should not be persecuted for it.

Stop persecuting other's because they look, sound, act and understand differently than you. Democracy does not mean we all believe the same thing.

It means we can all understand, act and live differently and still get along, as long as we do it like civilized human beings.

Abdul Alim Ibn Salahudeen

# New Era Publishing

## PRESENTS

## Terrorist In Brooklyn

### Revolutionary or Conspirator

*Written by: Anthony Brewer*

# PROLOGUE

*IRAQ, ONE YEAR EARLIER*

**All four men sat quietly staring at each other** through clouds of smoke that filled the room, bellowing from their overpriced Cohiba Robustos cigars. They glared at each other with mind bottling concentration as if each man could to read the thoughts of the other.

"We all have a decision to make," One man said with a Texan accent, breaking the silence.

He drew the attention of the other three men who locked their eyes on him and almost simultaneously took a toke off of their cigars thinking that it was the Senator who had a decision to make.

These men traveled halfway around the world to sit in attendance. Each man bringing a particular service that could contribute to the success of this endeavor, if the Senator committed once and for all to this project he called them to be a part of.

It was his project after all, but there were some particulars he was not in agreement with. Or was it those behind the curtain, who originally engineered this project that were not willing to blatantly put their signatures on it.

"The hard part is already done, Saddam Hussein is dead. The U.S. military is clearing the path for us to set up shop and literally thousands of men are signing up with Sheppard Private Military

Security as we speak," Carlton Richard advised. "And I am sure a continued presence here for the next what five years or so will aid our objective," Richard added.

Mr. Francis CEO and founder of Sheppard's Private Military Company sat quietly. Carlton Richards spoke for the both of them, his presence was enough. He was already established in Iraq.

In previous operations he worked hand and hand with U.S. military, being his staff was made up of largely 65% of retired Marines, Army and Air Force soldiers of all rankings up the latter to General.

Some particulars had to be ironed out and fast since the time table was already set and out of their control. In other words the usual question had to be answered, how far and to what peril would they go to achieve this objective.

Once this agreement was signed $80,000,000,000 would be sent to Iraq under the guise of troop support, rebuilding of Iraq or whatever legislation that was pending and logistically correct, compliments of Senator Borish's brother President Borish. The $80,000,000,000 would be enough to get the ball rolling and everyone involved and on the same page.

A knock on the door stole the attention and stares from the Senator. The door opened and a man and woman stood in the doorway. The man was about to enter the room until the woman placed her hand on his shoulder stopping him in his tracks. He looked at her expression then nodded in agreement.

He said something in Arabic only two men in the room really understood, Dercole a spook that spent his time in the trenches of at least seven countries as an agitator amongst warring militia factions and Francis who spoke six languages.

The woman stepped up but not beyond the threshold and translated, "He said that he was sorry but he does not smoke and would hope we could occupy another conference room."

All four men cordially nodded at each other in agreement. "Of course!" the Senator replied as he stood to greet his guest and lead them into another conference room only a few doors down.

"Mr. Talib Abdul Rahman it is a pleasure-" The Senator began by saying but stopped abruptly and extended his hand. "As saalamu alaikum," The Senator said as best his Texan accent would allow.

"Wa laikum!" Rahman replied shaking the Senator's hand.

The Senator's right eye brow rose and a mystified almost confused look appeared on his face that became a trademark of the Borish family when they were stumped by something. A news reporter once called it Borish junior's dumb look.

"How come my greeting sounder longer than yours?" He asked in Texan as if he too had his own foreign language. He really wanted to know what he said since everyone there knew the traditional reply was Wa alaikum as saalam.

Abdul Rahman's translator repeated the question to him in Arabic and he smiled nodding his head consenting for her to answer his question.

"Wa laikum means and to you." she began then explained that traditionally the recipient of the greeting would reply based on the intent of the person offering the salutations.

## ANTHONY BREWER

"It's a greeting of peace, what more intent do you need?" Carlton Richard asked as he stood to follow the Senator into the next conference room.

She had an answer for that as well but kept it to herself when she seen Talib Abdul Rahman eluding the question by turning and walking down the corridor in the direction of the vacant conference room he passed upon arriving.

Rahman knew this building well. He held several meetings there in the past of the same magnitude so it was safe for him to say he knew their intent. He was fully aware that the absence of governmental control in Iraq, the United Nation, Organization of the Petroleum Exporting Countries (OPEC) and however else had say so would shut the door and clamp down on all oil regulations allowing any outsider's control of Iraqi oil in a matter of a few days.

Barakata Oils owned by Talib Abdul Rahman was one of the largest preserves independent of OPEC that had a potential estimate of three trillion dollars once it got under U.S. control. But first they (the U.S. investors) had to get majority control, and they only had only a few days to do it.

Once Rahman seen all who were in attendance he knew their agenda. He knew of Carlton Richard oil mogul, Mr. Francis mercenaries, Mr. Dercole rebel rouser and the good old Senator who was a flunky for his brother Prseident Borish and the American interest.

The dialogue was brief but subtle since the tone was already set before the meeting. They all knew why they were there and that they only had a matter of days to sign a contract or agreement before the Arab Tribunal along with a United Nations passed laws that would ban any such contract giving outside interest, control and access to Iraqi oil.

## CHAPTER ONE

**Sleep comes less in the later years of a man's life**, be it single or married life. It's only when you're older that being single is more defined as being lonely. As for waking up 5:30 every morning like you had an alarm clock set in your head, is that loneliness magnified.

Waking up wide eyed and fully rested with nowhere to go and nothing to do, when the average Joe would just be turning over at 5:30 in their last stages of REM sleep and you could actually hear someone snoring if you listened.

Not waking up to a warm body next to him as of late Mr. Black Sr. has learned to adapt. He was beyond the stage of tossing and turning trying to will himself back to sleep. It was a steady transition starting with him doing chores and fixing things around the house before he went to work at his Youth Center.

After six months of that, his house in which he lived stayed immaculately polished. With every room repainted, fixture, ornament and gadget fixed and fully functional. Mr. Black Sr. decided to take his show on the road and move into the Youth Center. *Why not stay there and fix up the place a bit,* he convinced himself one morning while placing the coins from his loose change jar into rolls six o' clock in the morning.

After a few months in the Center and again with little to do, Mr. Black Sr. found himself meditating. It was not that separating mind from body kind of meditation. It was more like, I'm sitting here in the dark with a cluster of unresolved thoughts and the healthiest description for it was meditation.

After pushing pass thoughts he has successfully avoided for a year till now, Mr. Black Sr. turned his attention to the radio alarm clock that sounded. The bright red digital numbers read 5:15 AM and as usual he missed the first five minutes of the radio talk show, or was it a news station that entertained him every morning as he prepared himself to begin his day.

Since he never heard the first five minutes of the program he never heard the name of the host. Almost as if planned Mr. Black Sr. always found himself in the shower at 5:55 as the show signed off. The name of the program or who hosted it didn't matter; it was that top secret information that only grass root organizations espoused and commercial networks denounced secretly that kept him tuning in.

Last week's broadcast highlighted how children were being forced into military service through promotional recruitment campaigns targeting minority High Schools and Colleges. The young adults would sign forms stating that they may be interested in learning more about serving in the military.

These forms are then construed as contracts when these young men and women decide against joining and they are threatened with prison for breaking a contract that never existed.

"Kidnapping" and "Abduction" were the words used by the host, but the message was clear to Mr. Black. The first thing he did upon hearing that story was cancel all speaking engagements scheduled was various military recruiters previously scheduled to appear at the Youth Center. In the same spirit, he passed the word to surrounding schools and concerned parents.

In another story the Hispanic community was outraged by new immigration practices and the legislation that supported it. In the last two months several raids have been contrived nationwide with the intent of NOT returning the immigrants to their place of origin, but instead to a jail cell where they're charged with felonies and fined.

These measures according to the Latino World Watch, is primarily to aid the struggling economy with cheap labor in prison factories. Boosting the prison population by filling prison beds at a time when crime is down 14%. Saving the stocks and the jobs of those employed at the prisons that would otherwise be closed in suburban communities that need those jobs to survive.

"It's a revolving door-" Melinda Carrillo commented after her release, "they hire us by the bus load in American factories where they make big profits off of us. Then out of nowhere there is a raid and hundreds of us are arrested, but now instead of sending us back to our country, they take us to prison and have us working in more factories where they pay us nothing and make even more profit off of us. We only seek a fair days wage for a fair days work. Is this no longer what is true in America?"

"Sounds like she took it way back to the chain gang days." The host said adding his own little commentary, "At least that's how they filled prisons and got cheap labor back then to work the roads and highways. The flip side of that coin is the Hispanic community is predicted to outnumber the African American community in the next decade or so. So it sounds to me like the system that has been profiting off of the African American as a prison commodity for over a century now, are looking to profit off of the Hispanics in the same fashion and at the same time act out some form of subversive population and boarder control."

Supreme Court's verdict acquitting the detectives in the cold blooded murder of Kevin Dell was old news. But it still made you sick when you were reminded how the Dell family still struggled for justice, despite the fact Kevin was unarmed when he was shot down in a hail of bullets.

Three years gone by and Ms. Dell was taking responsibility for her son's death, "I taught my three sons to respect police and people in authority. Because of my teachings, my son stood idly by and allowed the police to shoot him down in cold blood. I have two other children left, and there is no need for me to tell you how I now instruct them...

But what I will tell you is that I am tired of turning on my television and hearing about our children being shot down in the streets by the same police we pay our tax dollars to protect them."

Mr. Black Sr. drifted off for a moment into his own thoughts on the topic and felt fortunate he was saved from such pain of losing a child. Losing his only child would have resulted in a war if someone so casually had taken his life as these police were doing today.

The word "Iraq" brought Mr. Black Sr. from his drift. "The first American oil company in history with headquarters operating in a foreign country, "The Disc Jockey repeated to emphasize who was winning in this war on terror.

Mr. Black didn't appreciate the commentary, in fact that was his cue to head for the shower. What did hold his attention as he made his way to the bathroom was the timing of this story the very same morning he woke with troubled thoughts of his wife and how she died in Iraq. For some reason this coincidence suddenly felt like an omen.

For the last past year or so you could set your clock by Mr. Black Sr. who has opened the B Street Youth Center seven days a week at 7:30 AM on the dot, that's when office hours began. A parent, a teacher or one of the youth that frequented the Center usually were standing there when he pulled the gate up. This morning it was Richard Jefferies.

When he seen the young man he smiled. He had not seen Jefferies for months so he knew this was going to cost him something. "Boy what are you doing standing outside my place of business. I hope you are not stalking me?"

Jefferies hopped off the mail box he sat on for the last fifteen minutes, watching people go to and from the train station on the corner. He pulled up his sagging pants with one hand and pulled a copy of the New York Times from under his arm with the other hand.

"Oh now its stalking Mr. B, but when you need me to pass out flyers-"

"Stop being so sensitive boy. That's for me?" Mr. Black Sr. asked surprised as he reached out for the paper.

"Yes sir. I know you like your paper so I figured-"

"Wait a minute, yes sir and you figured?" Mr. Black Sr. interrupted because at that point Jefferies made it clear what was becoming obvious. "Spit out kid I have places to go people to see." Jefferies handed Mr. B his paper and came clean. As it turned out Jefferies was suspended from school yesterday for his extra curriculum activities that ranged from cutting class, smoking reefer, forging documents and the list went on but Jefferies biggest problem was that he didn't tell his parents he was suspended.

Mr. B laughed as he waved to his neighbors and store owners as he made his way to his breakfast spot. "I am confused, you're suspended and I know you don't like school so enjoy the vacation. I don't see a problem."

"The problem is there is too much going on in my house right now, so telling my peeps I am on vacation is not an option."

As soon as Mr. Black Sr. opened the restaurant door his eyes subconsciously glanced over to his spot in the corner. "I see you have company." The cook asked on seeing the little boy trailing Mr. Black.

"Yes Martha found him on my door step, might as well feed him." He replied as he walked to his seat smiling and nodding at the customers he passed.

As soon as Mr. Black Sr. sat he pulled out a phone from inside of his jacket pocket and asked Jefferies how he wanted him to help with the problem. Jefferies response was simple, "Let's go to the school and make this go away so I can get back on my grind."

Mr. Black Sr. raised his finger to silence Jefferies as he listened into the phone. "Yes good morning this is Mr. Black. Oh fine thanks for asking and yourself? Yes I've heard something like that. Yes I do and I will return your property to you in one piece, no problem. Okay Bye."

When Mr. Black Sr. got off the phone Jefferies was on his phone bragging to what had to be his girlfriend, that he would see her in school today. Mr. Black looked at his watch then went to work on the plate Susan put before him and suggested Jefferies get off the phone and do the same.

Fifteen minutes later and to Jefferies dismay, they were on the train and on the way to midtown Manhattan. As for Jefferies being out of school, if they made it back to Brooklyn in time they could deal with that then.

United Freedom has sponsored B Street Youth Center for the past three years. Mr. Mathews served as Director of United Freedom and today's meeting between him and Mr. Black was to assure those checks kept coming.

Lately it has been a hassle getting into the United Freedom Building. Sudden security enhancements around the city have made entry into the simplest places a task. Mr. Black Sr. displayed his driver's license to the security guards and gave a nod, "The young guy is playing hooky with me today."

"You're bugging Mr. B, why you telling everybody?" Jefferies asked out of embarrassment.

"There are some things everybody need to know and you being out of school, playing hooky is one of them. Think about it, if everyone knew would you do it?"

"Hell no, somebody would rat me out to my peeps." Mr. Black smiled at Jefferies as they entered the elevator.

"You learn fast."

As usual Mr. Mathews was glad to see Mr. Black. Their meetings were routine. Mr. Mathews didn't bother looking over the stats of the work Mr. Black Sr. was doing at his Center, on the streets and in neighboring school.

Are you ready for this year's voter registration drive?" Mr. Mathew asked as he neatly tucked Mr. Black's folder in a file cabinet labeled Brooklyn Youth Street Center.

That was a good question because the voter's registration drive was the last thing on Mr. Black's mind since he canceled last year's registration drive due to a family tragedy. "So what are we voting for this year?" Mr. Black Sr. inquired.

"Anything with forward movement," Mr. Mathew replied.

"Does this forward movement have a name or a face?"

"I'm sure it does. Let's try it how we did it the year before last. Just set up shop and we'll send a few people down and they could handle it from there with the particulars."

His task was accepted with a smile. These registration drives were his way of giving back to United Freedom, you scratch my back I scratch yours. It was never any work for Mr. Black Sr. or his staff because they would send their own people with their own agenda. Something like sending the missionaries to the natives.

Educating them in their way, than giving them the right to vote and do their bidding.

Mr. Black Sr. was about to get up out of his seat when he was shaken back into it. "What the hell was that, another earthquake?" Mr. Mathew hollered. He ran into the receptionist area and Mr. Black Sr. followed looking for Jefferies.

The receptionist was on the floor on all four, scrambling for something firm to hold on to. Jefferies was planted in his seat holding on for dear life and no one knew what was going on or what to do.

The shaking stopped immediately. Mr. Mathew started looking around, he ran to the window but he was too high up to see the streets. He grabbed the phone called down to the front desk, after the $1^{st}$ ring, the $2^{nd,}$ by the $3^{rd}$ he thought the worse, it was an explosion and the whole bottom level was wiped out!

Mr. Black Sr. helped up the receptionist and looked at Mr. Mathew's face as he came out his office, it wasn't a good look. "What's going on?" He asked. To that Mr. Mathew could not give an answer. Mr. Black's eyes pivoted back and forth as he looked at the surrounding doors "Exit" he darted towards the exit and looked for a sign, a hint as to what just happened.

There was a little activity below but nothing alarming. Mr. Black Sr. turned to Mr. Mathews for any suggestions. When he seen Mathews wasn't taking control of the situation he did.

"I operate better on solid ground, at least until I know what's going on," He said, then turned to Jefferies and told him to stay on his heels as he invited Mr. Mathews and whatever stragglers to follow his lead.

In less than forty seconds the fifteenth floor was empty and they were in route to the first floor. Halfway down they encountered others trying to make a safe exit.

By the time they made it to the first floor lobby it was empty, not even security. As they made it through the revolving doors and onto the street they located the staff and other occupants of the United Freedom Building standing there in awe as they stared off to a distance at a building they just knew would crumble.

The crowd advanced as Mr. Black Sr. back peddled away from what he tried to avoid, what was obvious from the billowing black and gray smoke that towered above them.

"Oh shit Mr. B, we were that close to being blown up." Jefferies said as he turned to Mr. Black who was already a good five feet from the crowd and still going backwards. Until someone running towards the explosion almost mowed him down, snapping him out his stupor.

Mr. Black Sr. regained his senses and moved forward tapping Jefferies on his shoulder. Then he found Mr. Mathew to finish their business, than he headed back to Brooklyn as fast as he could.

As bad as Mr. Black Sr. wanted to get back to Brooklyn and hide behind closed doors he couldn't, he still had Jefferies that meant another stop.

From the moment they got off the train the explosion in midtown Manhattan was the topic on everyone's lips. People stood in bunches as they chitter chattered repeating whatever bits and pieces of the breaking news bulletins dispatched. Jefferies couldn't wait to get into school and tell his friends he was only a few buildings away from a terror attack and give his version of what happened.

When they walked into the Principal's office, everyone was busy calling their love ones who they thought would have or could have been in the area of the explosion. The rest talked amongst themselves as they worked and listened to radio reports of what transpired. Listening to the conversations Mr. Black thought to call Jefferies parents and tell them he was safe, but once Mr. Black seen the Principal he told Jefferies to have a seat and do it himself.

The conversation with the Principal didn't last long since both men had more serious issues on their minds, and with the present trend of activities it would be safer for Jefferies in school. The Principal let Mr. Black Sr. off without the usual tallying of the favor bank and they departed.

The old timer had to make his escape, get away, seclude himself. He went to the one place he knew he could get away and no one knew his name or his grief.

It was a pilgrimage to a sacred place that he hasn't visited in a long while. He entered the park in his usual manner through the rear entrance then followed the maze that led to the pond. He then circumvented it seven times and sat on a bench where he and his wife used to sit. He crossed his legs as he searched for a comfort zone and watched the people pass, then he took a walk down memory lane.

## CHAPTER TWO

**"Agent Black please come quickly, you should see this,"** An agent shouted from the doorway he occupied. Agent Black slowly raised his hand then stuck out a finger to indicate one moment.

He removed his glove off of his left hand. "Mr. Kodak, take a shot of this," Agent Black instructed pointing to a pile of rubble revealing wires mixed with the debris that sat at the base of one of six pillars that supported the building. As soon as the camera snapped a shot of the targeted area, Mr. Black carefully picked up a small plastic device, placed it in a latex glove and put it in his pocket.

Agent Black stepped through the debris and followed the agent to a lower level that contained wiring for most of the buildings electrical system. They made it around and through the debris to a pillar where another agent and two uniform police officers stood.

Agent Black reached out for the flash light the officer was holding he took it. He shined it around the basement from where he stood looking at the pillar from the base all the way up to the ceiling, than back down to its base again where he pulled a pen out and began ciphering through a pile of debris.

"Over here Mr. Kodak." Agent Black pointed to the area he wanted a shot of that contained the same material found on the upper level. "Does this building have eyes?" Agent Black asked Agent Brinsky who was standing by awaiting instruction from the senior agent.

ANTHONY BREWER

"According to the information I have received-" Agent Black raised his hand then the finger popped out. "One word yes or no."

"Yes"

"Where?"

Agent Brinsky waved a piece of paper she held in her hand that she scribbled a name, address and department. She handed it to Agent Black who looked at it and gave it back to Agent Brinsky.

"Good work, you lead I'll follow."

On the way to the Trocoby Building Agent Black apologized to Agent Brinsky for the hand gesture but explained to the junior agent that their unit was responsible for a follow up after every terrorist action. "Our response has to be immediate so the trail is still hot and the bad guys are still in town, so every second counts in word and action."

The Trocoby Building is the Central headquarters for the Lynstone Building that was attacked 9:25 that morning, and seven other branches spread out across the country. The Trocoby Building is owned by Cortex Industries, a billion dollar international conglomerate that handled affairs in at least sixteen countries.

"Federal Agents Brinsky and Black here to see Mr. Filler Interdepartmental Surveillance." Agent Brinsky said as she flashed his badge at the lobby security waiting to be pointed in one direction or another.

"Yes Agent Brinsky, Agent Black I was expecting you." Mr. Filler called out as he made his way down the corridor.

Mr. Filler exchanged handshakes with the agents then directed them to what he described as Fillervision. Anytime Mr. Filler welcomed visitors to view his work place for the first time, he introduced it with pride.

As he opened the door he looked at the agents faces to see if they were impressed, that first reaction meant everything to him. Agent Brinsky's face lit up like a kid at an arcade. No fault of her own, that's how the place looked with all the screens in high pitch colors. Agent Blacks facial expression was unchanged, he was not impressed.

Mr. Filler began by giving the agents a tour. Each section of monitors were set up like islands, designated for surveillance of seven of Cortex's Corporations.

Since the sudden increase of terror attacks of their corporations investing in foreign policy, the Trocoby Building was only responsible for the surveillance of their east coast branches.

Once Agent Black got a feel of the surveillance set up he ended the tour. "I need you to pull up the footage from the Lynstone Building at 6:00 AM in the lobby. "

"Are you looking for something specific?" Mr. Filler asked anxious to show off the advances of Fillervision technology. Agent Black paused long enough to consider the request. "From the time of the explosion I need a replay of the lobby, the lower level and the main entrance on each monitor."

Mr. Filler punched something into his keyboard transferring the information to another station. That station consisted of one large screen that displayed a total of twenty multiple screens each showing an area in the Lynstone Building.

"You said the lobby?"

They looked up at the large monitor, the number displayed was #5, the main entrance was #1 and so on. Now Agent Black understood the layout seeing each camera had its own screen. They could actually watch every section in the building at one time.

Seeing how the building was laid out from a computer projected hologram of the buildings blueprint Agent Black focused on the hot spots. "Give me 17, 21, 22, 26 and 36 as well." Mr. Filler complied and punched in the numbers, the time and hit the search button.

The images appeared on the monitor closest to Agent Brinsky at the exact time of the explosion. The blast suddenly appeared on the screen in Hi-Definition, with crystal clear audio slightly startling Agent Brinsky. Agent Black took his eye off the monitor for a second just to give Filler a look.

The large screens were something to see, that very moment the explosion and how everyone reacted throughout the building all on one screen. Then just as Agent Black suspected, monitor #5 right there in the lobby was where everything unfolded.

Mr. Filler and both agents froze at the sight of the altercation. A man dressed in a service technician uniform was confronted by a security guard inquiring about work being done in the lobby during one of its busiest hours. The technician tried to explain but the security guard was unyielding. Agitated the technician turned away from the guard to go his way until the guard grabbed the technician by the shoulder.

"Show me your authorization, I mean your work permit." The guard stammered nervously as the technician turned to him.

"Here is my authorization," The technician said holding a revolver. "Bang" "Bang" "Bang", the shots rang out throughout the lobby causing everyone to scramble and run leaving the technician with no other option and no more time to finish his work .

He discharged the last three rounds in his revolver at the second security guard rushing at him to buy him time and pull a gadget out of his canvas shoulder bag he was carrying.

Unbeknown to the guard who was successful in tackling the technician to the ground, the gadget he managed to retrieve from his bag was a detonator. Neither of them hit the floor in one piece and that charge triggered more explosives.

Agent Black had Mr. Filler back tracked to the time he entered the building then trailed him to the moment of the explosion. He entered the building with another man.

The second man was among the survivors and remained in the building until it was being evacuated and then he made his move and got out with the crowd.

The surveillance camera connected to an adjacent building helped them pin point a man leaving with the crowd dressed in a uniform identical to the technician in the lobby who blew himself to pieces. Now the agents had a face and license plate number of the service truck he hopped into.

Agent Black had the information transferred to FBI Headquarters. By the time they arrived at Headquarters the information was already analyzed and Agent Black's tactical team was on standby waiting to be prepped.

Agent Black had a five man team that worked in close proximity. Agent Jenkins the sniper, Agent Walton the bomb specialist, Agent Simms Mr. International, Agent McCarthy the veteran and Agent Brinsky the rookie. One of several counter terrorist teams put together to respond to the increased attacks on America and its allies.

The man in the main lobby was Jalal Ibn Sandi a contractor. His accomplish was Idris Ibn Sandi a chemical engineer and Jalal's younger brother. These were not the run of the mill criminals who rented a truck in a made up name, it was registered to Sandi's Contracting Company.

Before the read out came back with the address, the tactical team was already in route. They made it to their destination in fifteen minutes and were waiting for the word go. The bomb squad and local support was a block off laying in the cut.

The van they traced was parked in front of the house, the quick response time could actually have paid off. Agent Black couldn't put all his eggs in one basket so he and Agent Brinsky stayed back with a "Plan B".

Agent Black was reluctant to act hastily. He wanted to be there, from where he sat at headquarters he felt he was missing something and with the two minute profile he put together chances were he did.

With two brothers involved there were too many variables, like a whole family of mad bombers for starters. But the one thing he knew for sure with one brother dead and the other still out there, he had to do something quick. It was only a matter of time before the illusive one regrouped and reappeared to do more damage than the failed first attack.

Agent Brinsky watched the perplexed look on Agent Black's face while she tried to figure why he hesitated to give the order for them to go in. "Send in the old ghost and give him long distance cover," Agent Black ordered in a slow reluctant voice.

That was Agent Blacks way of playing it safe. They called McCarthy a ghost because that's how he moved slowly, he would come and go without being seen and he missed very little.

Simms, Walton and Jenkins moved into position. Simms came from the east, Walton came from the west and Jenkins went north. Once McCarthy seen Simms and Walton emerging from both ends of the block he already knew his long distance cover was in place.

McCarthy walked past the contractor van and inspected its content on his way to the house. It was a small one family home with two floors. The windows were clean but shaded with thin curtains allowing him to see from the front of the house to where a wall carrying a portrait of colorful flowers barred his vision.

As he approached the house he visually searched for his entry point without looking directly at it. It was a well kept house which made it harder to figure as to what to expect. The two colonial glass doors guaranteed easy access that he passed up and opted for the walkway on the side of the house. There where three trash cans neatly positioned under an open window.

'*A gift.*' he thought as a smirk appeared on his face and his words of wisdom he usually departed came to mind. The first rule is never breach, you breach they teach.

## ANTHONY BREWER

Breach a dwelling of a known bomber and chances are you trigger a booby trap or alert some guy with a bomb strapped to him. "Going window shopping," McCarthy whispered as he dipped into the walkway.

"I got a better view." Jenkins replied as he covered McCarthy from a distance with his sniper rifle. Jenkins was able to see from the second floor window to the next room and the first two rooms of the first floor. "Entry point clear." Jenkins confirmed as McCarthy agilely leaped up on the trash can and went through the window like he did it a hundred times before while at the same time his eyes scanning for breach cords, lasers or motion detectors.

When he didn't see any booby traps he looked around for a nervous guy with sweaty palms and a bomb attached to him. "Clear," McCarthy whispered as he drew his side arm and made his way through the house. There was a blind spot for Jenkins, he could not see what made Agent McCarthy stop in his tracks as he entered the next room.

There was a short stocky person sitting in a chair with a shoe box on his lap and he had his hand in the box as he slowly looked up at McCarthy. McCarthy ignored Jenkins inquiries as to what made him stop so abruptly.

The young man raised his head to where he and McCarthy made full eye contact. He didn't seem alarmed or surprised by McCarthy's presence. The young man's eyes began to drift back and forth between the contents of the box that rested on his lap and McCarthy.

Jenkins saw something shoot pass his scope then disappeared, "There is something coming up behind you," He warned and aimlessly searched for what evaded detection thus far.

McCarthy quickly raised his gun and pointed it at the young man then placed his back against the wall. For the first time the young man spoke "Wait mister!" his voice gave McCarthy a hint of his age. In that second of distraction McCarthy turned to look at the boy then turned back to look for the third person, McCarthy would have jumped out of his skin if the young woman before him wasn't so beautiful.

She stood there side by side with McCarthy with her back against the wall as if she too was on guard from some unknown presence. McCarthy had to reposition himself because he stood between the two of them and couldn't watch them both.

He didn't want to make any sudden moves. She looked harmless as she stood there bare footed in a thin cotton skirt that reached down to her ankles and a bright yellow tee shirt that read "Sunshine" on the front of it.

She was slightly distracted by McCarthy's gun but her focus was on the shoe box in her brother's lap. McCarthy slowly holstered his side arm. The young lady responded to his gesture with a half smile, then swiftly walked over to her younger brother who was twice her size and gave him a scolding look as she extended her hands.

His calm face with his chubby cheeks suddenly burned red and turned into a look of embarrassment. He reluctantly handed her the shoe box, then gave Agent McCarthy a glance before putting his head down in shame.

She carefully placed the box on the table then bent over to pick up the boxes cover from the floor. Finally, the contents of the box was exposed to McCarthy. He took a step forward to get a better look.

When she seen his interest in the box she quickly covered it with the lid. "Why do you and those other people come through our window?" the girl asked.

"Are you the only ones here?" McCarthy retorted.

"Yes," She replied and was confirmed not even a second later by Simms. McCarthy had several questions. How did she know others came through the window when she was standing next to him in a blind spot? Why wasn't she startled by his presence, his gun?

Instead he pulled out a photo, "Does this man live here?" he asked showing here a photo of Idris Ibn Sandi the younger of the two brothers that escaped. She responded with a few sure nods as she looked McCarthy over as if she expected an answer to her question.

"Do you know where he is? McCarthy asked this time looking at the boy hoping he would answer. She looked at her little brother then shook her head. "No" she replied almost annoyed as if she knew Agents Simms and Walton were searching the house while McCarthy questioned her.

## TERRORIST IN BROOKLYN

The young ladies name was Tinsia, she was eighteen years of age and her brother Talib was twelve. He was just big for his age thanks to his new found love, American fast food.

They moved from Iraq less than a year ago when their parents were murdered for refusing to sell their oil business. Their surviving family abroad and in the United States was told that they died as a result of an Iraqi military operation gone wrong.

An eye witness to the murders saw differently but of course Tinsia didn't tell the agent any of that she just sat there and periodically shook her head or nodded from question to question.

Special Agent Black told them they were taking too much time. It was time to pull out and let the secondary unit take it from there. Simms, McCarthy and Walton left the house leaving the secondary unit to take over.

McCarthy made a U-turn and went back into the house. If neither of the kids knew about their uncles plans to carry out today's attack, why was Talib holding onto the box with his uncles possessions like he knew his uncle would not be coming back.

McCarthy went in looking for Talib because he knew for some reason Tinsia was too smart to give him any useful information.

While Tinsia was being questioned by one of the secondary agents, her brother was taking to a snack to wear off the pressure of police and their questions about his family.

From the corner of her eye Tinsia saw McCarthy heading into the kitchen where her little brother was. She called out to him and told him something in Arabic.

McCarthy couldn't understand what she said but whatever she said, he seen Talib rush pass him with snacks in hand and sat beside his sister.

McCarthy looked at the agent who was questioning Tinsia for a translation. "Fasting is a restraint of the mouth." The agent translated, when she seen McCarthy didn't grasp it the agent broke it down. "She threatened him, if he spoke to you she would starve him."

McCarthy stood in the doorway smitten with disbelief as all the thoughts registered at once in his mind's eye. How Tinsia crept up on him without him having a clue. That calm look she had finding a strange man in her house with a gun.

She even detected the rest of the team entering her house before he did. To a veteran these things should have drawn a flag that made him look beyond her bright colors and innocent exterior, what if she had the gun?

McCarthy started thinking about the propaganda reports of militia groups that trained children in countries like Iraq and Afghanistan. McCarthy looked at bare footed Tinsia who didn't look no older than his twelve year old granddaughter, then glanced over at chubby cheeked Talib who sat quietly next to his sister clinching onto his snacks and watching McCarthy. McCarthy shook it off then went to catch up with the rest of the team.

## CHAPTER THREE

"**Peace be unto you,**" The voice on the other end of the phone greeted.

"And to you!" Sandi replied.

"I call with news that a very good friend of ours is here carrying on business as usual," The man said. Those words left Sandi muddle headed. Up until that moment Sandi was positive Mr. Carlton Richard owner of Cortex was not only in New York, but was scheduled to appear at the Lynstone Building earlier that morning.

"Are you sure?" Sandi inquired.

"As sure as the sun is to rise on the east and set in the west, but I must go time and opportunity is upon us."

"Wait please wait, Jalal has gone back to God."

"From God we come to God we must return, but this is even an opportunity you missed."

"And by God it an opportunity I deserve above all," Sandi demanded in anger as he reached his destination. The phone was quiet for a moment, "May you get what you strive for." The voice replied then the phone went dead as Sandi parked his car in a spot marked "Reserved Parking Only".

Sandi parked his navy blue Mercedes Benz and slowly looked around as he climbed out of his car. When he seen no one was in sight he reached back into the car and opened the hood and the trunk of the car.

He quickly went to the front of the car, disconnected the car battery then attached to it two long cable wires that traveled throughout the car and stopped in the trunk of the car. Each cable was connected to two separate customized cases that took up the length and width of the spacious trunk.

With one gentle touch of a button one case quickly opened after the other. At the sound of footsteps Sandi quickly reached into each case, flipped a switch and closed both cases. He then grabbed a rag from the trunk and calmly closed it as he turned to see who was approaching.

"Good evening sir," Parking security announced as he glanced at his watch to confirm the time "Coming or going?" he asked.

Sandi gave a half smile as he began to wipe down his car. "Just getting in," Sandi replied then winked at the attendant, "I can't help it, every time I leave her behind I have to wipe her down."

"Yes it's a pretty blue but I hate to be the one to tell you, this is reserved parking only."

"Yes I know and unfortunately I will be working late." Sandi informed him as he tossed the rag into his car and pulled out his brief case. Sandi asked the attendant to keep an eye on his baby as he headed towards elevator without any further discussion about the parking. He came up in the elevator to the first floor and left out the main entrance where he jumped into a cab and headed straight for the airport.

Sandi knew he wouldn't be able to go back home so he had everything he needed in his brief case. Sandi had two passports and flight plans already set up for him and his brother to leave the country if everything went as planned. The only problem it didn't, his brother was dead and by now he had to assume his identity was known.

He discarded him and his brother's passports and used Steven Whitherpool's passport. Whitherpool was an American professor who bore a remarkable resemblance minus Sandi's slightly darker complexion, but it was their dark eyes and well kept beards that made their oval faces match.

The only problem, he never booked a flight in Whitherpool's name and all flights leaving within the hour were booked solid.

The sudden cancellation on the only flight leaving within minutes made Sandi feel that was an act of God. Now the only thing remained was for him to pick up the tickets for his flight. His hands began to sweat as he stood on line holding this passport that was not his own.

In all his thirty something years on God's planet Sandi never commit a crime. Suddenly questions flashed through his head. Where was Whitherpool? Was he in America or abroad? Is this fraud or identity theft or both?

As the line moved closer Sandi's alarm went off on his watch, it was time. He quickly raised his hands to his face, closed his eyes and said what appeared to be a prayer that was interrupted by someone on line behind him.

"Never flown before ha?"

Sandi said "Amin" quietly to himself and turned to the brightly dressed, high spirited young lady who was eagerly awaiting an answer. "Every time is like my first time," Sandi replied.

"Look at you, you're sweating," She observed pointing at his forehead with one hand and reaching into her bag with the other, handing him what looked like a pink handkerchief.

"Don't worry, once we're in the air it won't be so bad. Now go on your next," She said ushering Sandi forward. Sandi took the handkerchief, thanked her and told her to go next as if he was returning the kind gesture.

He needed that moment to pull himself together and that moment came and gone too fast. It was again time for him to step up to the plate.

If he was too nervous that would draw a flag and the fact that he was and looked like an Arab didn't help matters. He licked his dry lips, mustered up a smile and approached with passport in hand.

The reservationist took his passport, punched something into her keyboard waited a moment then smiled.    "Mr. Whitherpool lucky of you catching that cancelation as you did."

At that very moment, before she reached for his ticket or inspected the passport a scream echoed through the airport. "Oh my God!"

Everyone turned simultaneously towards the scream. It was a woman standing in front of an elevated television set, looking up with terror in her eyes. People quickly gathered around her. Airport Security and Management responded by moving things along by saying everything was alright.

The last thing they needed at an airport was panic about an explosion that had nothing to do with them. All interdepartmental communications instructed that all airport employees continued processing and insisted that they pick up the pace before people started canceling flights, as they often did when word of an explosion surfaced.

"What is it?" Sandi asked the reservationist. "I don't know," She responded as she was trained. Never use the words bomb, explosion, hijacking or anything that can create enough panic in a person that would cause them to cancel or postpone their flight. She picked up the pace stamping and handing Sandi back his passport, his ticket and shouting "Next, please next."

In no time Sandi was on his flight being directed to his seat. To his surprise he was seated right next the young lady he seen on line. She looked up at Sandi "Are you following me mister?" She asked in a loud voice drawing attention to Sandi. Even the stewardess who escorted Sandi to his seat became concerned until the young lady laughed at the nervous look on Sandi's face.

"I should be ashamed of myself right, already knowing how hard it is for you to fly."

Sandi let out a sigh of relief as he took his seat and the young lady asked him his name. "Please call me Professor-"

"And now your pulling rank on me!" she said starting back in on him. But this time Sandi realized that was part of her personality. For the first time in days Sandi smiled. She introduced herself as Crystal a student of international trade and foreign policy.

When Sandi arrived in Iraq, there was a car waiting for him that took him to a distant relative's house that he hasn't visited in years. He was greeted by an old uncle and aunt who only spoke to him briefly than left him sitting alone.

The way everything went so far he thought his companions made the arrangements and would meet him there and update him on their next mode of attack. Instead a woman entered the room. He couldn't tell who she was until she stood before him and removed her veil.

This was the first time he seen his intended in over a year since all this began. Sandi quickly looked away and tried to put a distance between him and her.

"Iqy stop and look at me," She demanded.

"How cold your brother betray me like this?"

"He loves you. He loved your brother, father and sister as if they were his own and now your brother is dead Iqy. You are all we have from a whole family. You are all I have." She started to pull him into her, "And I am not going to lose you because of oil."

"Nonsense Fatima, this is not about oil, they killed my family, my relatives. I couldn't even give them a burial because they couldn't find their bodies and you say this is about oil, **this is about qisas.**"

"What is retribution when you too are dead. You promised to wed me. I have rights over your qisas," She scorned as she began to cry and hugged him tightly pleading with him.

He was suddenly ambushed by the scent of her body, its softness and her crying in his ear. He could not help but hold her as tight as she held him. She stopped crying and all the fight left him, he was captured by her heavenly embrace.

"Fatima!" he yelled as he yanked himself out of her arms, "Surely if a man and a woman are alone in a room Satan is the third party with temptation."

Fatima's lip curled and her eyes squinted, "The devil and temptation is what you speak of when I mention our marriage?" She was infuriated by his statement. Before he could reply, "Pow" she slapped him then started crying again.

He didn't know what to say to appease her rage. What could he say, she was right. Up until the day his family was killed, she gave up everything in her preparation for her move to America once they got married. The only thing they got since was further apart but she still waited patiently. Fatima has been keeping tabs on Sandi through her brother Omar who has pledged to help Sandi seek qisas.

All was good for Sandi until Omar joined a fundamentalist group of Muslims against western occupation in Iraq. Fatima begged her brother to abandon Sandi with hopes he would give up and start a new family with her. She was convinced if he carried on in America by himself he would be killed.

Sandi agreed and told her he did not want to die in a distant land alone. He wanted and needed more than anything to begin a family of his own and that's why he came back to finish this with the help of her brother.

## CHAPTER FOUR

**Now he had to find Omar** because Fatima refused to tell him where he could be found. Noontime was approaching and he had an idea where he could find his would be brother in law and long time companion. Despite Fatima's pleading for him to stay he wasted no time, he made his way to the Mosque. This way he would be able to catch Omar before they dispersed from noon prayer.

As Sandi approached the Mosque he heard the call to prayer. He began to relax as the nostalgia started to set in, as if Fatima's warm embrace wasn't enough. The voice of the small man saying come to prayer was like his welcome back home. Sandi smiled and nodded at the familiar faces passing him on their way to prayer as he took off his shoes and socks to perform abolution.

As the majority of the praying congregation departed Sandi sat in personal prayer, praying for his mother, father, sister and brother. He prayed that their graves be spacious and that their souls were greeted at the gates of heaven.

He went on about paradise and its beauty, the prayer rolled off his tongue like poetry from saying it repetitiously for the last year. Half way through the prayer Sandi paused, his eyes opened only slightly as he looked into his empty palms cupped before him.

He bit down on his back teeth and grimaced "Ya Allah, surely man loves a thing that is evil and bears no fruit and hates a thing that is good and profits his soul. Surely fighting to enjoin for what is right is prescribed for the good of mankind and his soul. Please raise from amongst me a band of men who will support my cause to enjoin what is right and punish those who are wrong, Amin."

As he sat there and the thought of his supplication resonated through his body he felt his whole resolve changed. By the time he regained his composure he realized more than half of the people already exited the Mosque and not yet has he seen one of his companions.

He quickly grabbed his shoes and socks and stumbled into the courtyard as he fixed his clothes.

Anxiety set in and Sandi began to feel panic. People began to greet him that he hasn't seen in the past year. He bounced from person to person returning the ceremonial greeting and embrace as his eyes searched beyond the warm smiles and hugs.

"Iqbal" a voice called out. Sandi turned to his left, then to his right as he searched for that voice that seemed like a life line. "Uthman my beloved," Sandi proclaimed as he went to Uthman with open arms. Uthman was a childhood friend of Sandi and his sister. Uthman was an old fashion, more traditional Muslim whose business was trade, his living and way of life modest.

In the thirteen years as a merchant Uthman amassed quite a bit of wealth and political influence. It has always been his theory that they go hand and hand, that's why he always encouraged other Muslims to become politically aware how politics abroad influence Iraq.

Uthman hasn't seen his old friend in a while, but since bad news traveled fast he was already informed of Jalal's fate. Uthman looked into Sandi's heavy worn eyes and invited him to an eatery they would meet at during their latter school years.

"That would be a treat but-" Sandi began his reply to be cut short by Uthman, "But, Iqbal Idris Sandi you have never turned down a free meal and it would be an insult if you broke the tradition at my bidding." On that note Sandi looked at Uthman with a smirk of entrapment.

In no time they were sitting before a spread sharing lamb as Sandi sat patiently listening to Uthman update him on his business ventures, his twelve kids and whatever other useless information Uthman thought Sandi did not want to hear.

The eatery was filled with people eating lunch and socializing. The big flat screen television carried news reports from al Jazero, mostly local news from that area.

At Sandi's request the waitress changed the channel to BBC International news. World sports, then there was news on the western occupation in Iraq. After five minutes nothing, disappointed he excused himself and went to the bathroom.

Sandi wasn't looking for recognition. He just wanted to be appraised of the damage done to Cortex Industries. He needed something to speak towards his efforts in America against his family's killers.

The second building he blew up before his flight was one of Cortexes smaller buildings. With what he had to work with, the time he had to do it in and the fact that he was alone left him no choice unless he wanted to be reckless and disregard the body count.

He could have placed the same explosives in any of Cortexes larger buildings and there were many to choose from. Access to those at midday when the casualties would have been highest and the killing of hundreds of innocent people was one thing he was trying to avoid. In his mind there was a fine line between revenge and becoming like the terrorist corporation he wanted to put out of business.

When Sandi exited the bathroom he stood in the doorway as the squeaky door closed behind him. He took a deep breath and headed down the narrow hallway leading back into the dining area. As he passed a pay phone Omar's name came to mind. A short plump man who was balding badly, was back peddling trying to get to the phone while still watching television backed up into Sandi.

The man offered a grim look as he struggled to take his eye off of the television long enough to apologize. As soon as he made eye contact with Sandi the man's eyes began to flutter. He turned his head back and forth to compare Sandi to the face on the big screen television.

Sandi more interested with what the man was looking at then his apology, took one quick agile step sliding pass the man and there it was right in his face, Sandi's jaw dropped.

"Sandi" Uthman called out and everyone looked at Uthman then in the direction he was looking. It was then that Uthman realized calling out Sandi's name wasn't a smart move. People started pointing and the whispers began.

Sandi ignored everyone as he walked towards the television like he was in a trance. Before he knew it he was standing face to face with himself.

Uthman knew it would be a matter of time before someone called the police or worse, flagged a soldier. He paid for the food then tried to pull Sandi from in front of the television. "We must go, now." Uthman instructed as he grabbed Sandi's arm.

"No, this is not me," Sandi replied jerking his arm away from Uthman.

"Foolishness, it is you down to your crooked tooth."

Sandi moved closer to the television and continued to listen to the reports as it gave more details.

"The numbers are coming in, but it's still not clear. We spoke to the spokesman at Cortex International and we are told anywhere from 55 to 70 of their employees were working in this building behind me when the explosion went off." The reporter gestured over her shoulder at the building, fire trucks and ambulances.

Shattered glass, hurt and disoriented people disbursed for as far as the camera could see and people were still being evacuated from the building. "Wait a minute ladies and gentlemen, we have more information, the suspected terrorist responsible for what you see here-"

Sandi snapped out of his trance long enough to glance around at the people in the diner as they whispered amongst themselves. They tried to put the news flashes in prospective and peeped shyly at Sandi.

## TERRORIST IN BROOKLYN

"Look!" a man pointed with one hand at the television while holding his cell phone in the other hand.

It was surveillance video feedback of a parking garage being shown. There was a close up shot of a blue Mercedes Benz. The silence in the diner gave way to gasping sounds as the people watched in disbelief as a man stood emerging from the blue Benz, it was Sandi.

The reported directed everyone's attention to the time displayed on the lower left hand corner of the video, it read 4:31 PM less than an hour before the blast that occurred at 5:20.

Simultaneously everyone looked at their watches. Those who traveled back and forth to the United States quickly did the math, but those who were not frequent fliers or didn't know the difference in time zones were stuck like they had a pop quiz they didn't study for.

Before Uthman could grab Sandi and whist him away, the shabby tan paint that decorated the diner walls was quickly replaced by green uniforms. Soldiers systematically lined up around the interior of the restaurant surrounding everyone therein while holding their large automatic rifles.

Everyone sat in awe not knowing what to expect. A tall slinky man taking long strides walked into the diner and stopped in the center of the floor. He commanded so much attention that no one noticed the shorter thicker man who shamefully followed behind and stopped next to the tall man. He then extended his short pudgy arm in Sandi's direction with a finger pointing.

## ANTHONY BREWER

The dining room was quiet. All you could hear was the television ranting on as the tall man approached taking small steps to give himself time to look Sandi over.

He positioned himself in front of Sandi then looked over at his snitch for confirmation, at that very moment Sandi's face reappeared on the television set.

The tall man glared at the television with intense interest, only removing his eyes for a slight second to complete the identification. At that point he didn't need to hear any more. He took a step back and three soldiers quickly moved in on Sandi.

As quick as Uthman tried to jump between Sandi and the soldiers, he was knocked to the floor with the sharp blow to the head. He was head butted with an assault rifle. Likewise Sandi's struggle was of no avail, he was knocked unconscious and dragged away.

When Sandi came to his vision was blurry. He struggled to make out the figure of the man next to him. "I have been waiting patiently Mr. Sandi for you to regain consciousness. I am told you are a native."

Sandi listened to the voice until he was able to put a face to it. Once he realized it was the tall man from the diner Sandi tried to gain his composure as he looked out the window to see where he was.

"Do you recognize where you are?" The tall man asked watching Sandi look around. "I am Jama Raji, second in command of the newly elected police force and you couldn't have come at a better time."

# TERRORIST IN BROOKLYN

"Where is my companion?" Sandi asked breaking his silence.

"Hopefully he got off the floor and finished his meal." Raji replied with sarcasm.

"Where are you taking me?" Sandi asked forcefully. Raji ignored Sandi's question and continued on about the newly elected police force that didn't have the respect of the Iraqi people. Nor of the American government who didn't trust them because they thought they were in bed with terrorist groups with malefic intent towards the troops stationed in Iraq.

"But I assure you these misplaced suspicions will soon be replaced with countless benefits and privileges," He bolstered caught up in his own flatulence, until his mobile phone rang disrupting his speech.

He listened into the phone for a moment then turned and looked behind him, beside him and along the empty road that they traveled and seen nothing.

"I am Jama Raji, second in command and I will not threatened," Raji shouted into the phone then quickly hung up so he could notify the rest of his convoy.

He alerted the cars to his rear, then the car and truck ahead of him. As soon as the truck received its warning there appeared a man in the middle of the road flagging them to stop with a piece of white cloth in his hand.

"Don't stop you fool." The passenger yelled as the driver of the truck slowed down, then immediately picked up speed to accommodate the passenger.

The man standing in the middle of the road responded to the trucks sudden increase of speed by dropping to one knee and pulling a long instrument from over his shoulder and in the same motion, he balanced it on his shoulder and fired it. The truck came to a screeching halt trying to avoid the inevitable clash between the truck and the missile released from the rocket launcher.

"BOOM" The truck went flying into the air. The car behind it couldn't stop in time. The five and a half ton truck landed on the car crushing it, then incinerated its passengers almost simultaneously.

The rest of the convoy can to an uncontrollable stop. Clouds of dust rose and men who laid in ambush in the hinges emerged for their attack. They quickly surrounded the convoy then held their positions.

Jama Raji's door swung open and his long leg reached out for solid ground as he ejected himself out of his vehicle. That was all his soldiers needed to see, they all followed suit and jumped out of their vehicles. The attacking company did not budge, they maintained their positions.

Everyone's attention turned to the rear as three horses approached. One of the horses carried two men, the others just one. You could tell by the way the three men were dressed in all white garbs, heads wrapped and faces covered that the fourth man was not of them from his different dress, it was Uthamn.

Two horses stopped at a distance as the third horseman continued on to Jama Raji and demanded he turn over his prisoner.

From the response Raji gave it was evident the two men knew each other. "This is not an issue of politics. If you do not do as I command I will kill you and all your soldiers," The man on the horse demanded as he drew his weapon and all his men followed suit chambering their weapons and waited for the command.

Sandi slowly got out of the car. One of the lone horsemen from the rear galloped up to Sandi and extended his hand. Sandi looked into the eyes of the masked man then took his hand. Raji watched furiously as Sandi climbed onto the horse.

In a weak attempt to act like he had a choice in the matter Raji raised his hand signaling his soldiers to stand down. "This is something we both will regret," Raji promised.

"You should concern yourself more with your men before you look to police others Mr. Raji. I understand your men raided a small town north of Farda and killed a man and his child, amongst others. Why have they not been dealt with?"

"Khalil again you misunderstand. That situation has been addressed and those men dealt with," Raji said firmly.

Without replying Khalil turned his horse to the rear of Raji's convoy and approached the men that stood in the second to last group. All of Khalil's men held their position with the exception of four men that broke formation and followed as he went to address Raji's men.

Khalil climbed off his horse and walked between the small groups of men who tightly held their assault rifles with sweaty palms. "I am Khalil Yusuf al Salam. As explained to me by Jama Raji, I don't understand." Khalil looked over at Raji and pointed at him. "It is **he** who does not understand. If a man wants qisas for the lost of a family member or loved one, by Allah he is entitled."

As soon as Khalil said that, one of his men who broke formation and trailed behind Khalil took off his head wrap and face covering.

"Baqi Ibn Tarik brother of Basir Ibn Tarik, uncle of Omar Ibn Basir," Baqi announced loud enough for every man in the convoy to hear. Then he approached the man who he was told killed his nephew. "By God I seek retribution for my nephew, do you deny killing him?"

The man stuttered as he began to shake his head no. Before the man could get a full shake Baqi uttered "Bismi Allah" and the man's head rolled off the road into the hinges. Suddenly at the sight of this Sandi's rescue became trivial to him seeing this kind of justice executed.

Before Baqi could turn to the second man who was responsible for killing his brother the man farthest from him dropped to his knees. Khalil, Baqi and the rest of the men looked over to him.

"I am only a soldier. I only do as I am commanded, please call on your God you speak of for mercy," The man pleaded.

"You are a man first, you had a choice. You choose murder and because of you I have no brother." Baqi shouted as he raised his sword above his head.

"I bear witness in the one God!" The man quickly uttered.

"And his messenger?" Khalil asked from afar.

"Yes. Please have mercy?"

"Aarrghh" Baqi hollered as he swung his sword into the ground in rage.

Khalil placed his hand on Baqi's shoulder. "May Allah have as much mercy and forgiveness on you on the day of judgment." Then Khalil looked over at Raji. "When your day comes I will not be as merciful." Khalil said as he mounted his horse and went back the direction from which he came.

They made their retreat to a small town 20 miles outside of Baghdad in a small village its residents call Ardia. Omar introduced Sandi to Khalil and his companions. Everyone agreed Sandi needed no introduction, between what Omar already told them and all the media coverage he has been getting.

Everyone immediately busied themselves with one thing or another depending what they were doing before they were alerted of Sandi's abduction by Uthman and Omar insisted that they rescue him. Before Sandi could get Omar's full attention, Khalil whisked him away.

Sandi stood there in what looked like a warehouse, but the large petitions that stood as make shift walls altered the places appearance to make it look more like an office with over sized cubicles. He felt like he was in a maze, he couldn't see ten feet ahead in either direction without his view being obstructed by the petitions. '*Which way did he go?* Sandi asked himself as he struggled for a since of direction.

Sandi passed the first petition and seen two men hunched over a table. He moved in closer to see what they were doing. Sandi froze suddenly in his tracks at the sight of what appeared to be a bomb.

One of the men looked over his shoulder at Sandi. "I think its surplus." From the blank look on Sandi's face he figured Sandi didn't know what he was talking about so he carried on.

"Of course you, like many Americans don't know the reason for war. It is to unload billions of dollars of bombs and ammunitions," The man said as matter a factly as possible while giving Sandi a nod of the head then continued.

"Economics 101, use your supplies. Your budget gets you billions more and everyone profits but the innocent people they kill."

"Thanks for the economics lesson but what is wrong with that one?" Sandi asked peering at the bomb from a safe distance.

"Too much handling, some wires shaken loose." Shariff answered without looking up.

"Shariff's hobby is what you call in America?" the first man paused as he brainstormed for a word. He turned to Sandi, "When you buy an appliance that is no good and take it back. They in turn fix it and sell it again as new?"

There was a brief silence. "Refurbished?" Sandi asked and answered at the same time.

"Yes this is it. Shariff refurbishes American bombs as his hobby. Then we hear talk of how Iran supplies us with bombs."

Sandi looked inquisitively at the Arab that spoke better English then he did and thought about his views. "Who are you, what are you?" Sandi asked. The man laughed, "I am Basir, I was a journalist." Sandi nodded his head, that explained the English and the politics.

"What made you give up journalism?" Sandi asked.

"Shi'a Muslims and Sunni Muslims killing each other. Jews killing Muslims and Americans killing Muslims. I felt like an obituary columnist reporting the slaughter of Muslims.

Plus, American soldiers killing journalist for our reporting and bombing our radio stations. Then calling us agitators for speaking the truth about the genocide and war on Muslims, kind of helped me towards an early retirement."

Sandi took a step closer to the bomb. From the shape and design it was obvious a missile of some sort. Sandi remained quiet as he imagined the damage a missile five feet in length and 29 inches in diameter could do. Then he began to think about his family.

After a few adjustments Sheriff converted the U.S. missile into a remote activated bomb. Sandi did not think this kind of conversion could be done.

The call to prayer carried through the warehouse. Men began converging towards the musella in the center of the warehouse where everyone prayed with the exception of a few men who secured the perimeter. Once the Muezzin finished the first call to prayer Khalil addressed the Muslims with information acquired from other groups of Muslims stationed throughout Iraq with similar objectives.

A cease fire was being negotiated throughout Iraq between the Sunni and Shi'a Muslims. Most of the casualties amongst the militia groups have been due to sectarian wars. The truce amongst the tribal leaders would then free them to focus on the self governing of Iraq and the removal of American soldiers and private contractors.

"I agree we can take on a common goal to obtain peace in Iraq. Especially since America is looking to go elsewhere, like deeper into Afghanistan or into Iran. But there are still groups loyal to U.S. money and influence. They will not agree to a cease fire, it's not in their best interest," Basir insisted.

Khalil sat quietly gently stroking his long graying beard. Having already considered this fact, he was not in a position to say anything about it so he remained silent. The consensus amongst the overall body of Muslims was a cease fire so that was the instructions given to his men.

Sandi sat and listened, not fully aware of the politics between the Sunni and Shi'a militia in Iraq but he was able to discern that neither group had his objective in mind. In fact to the contrary a cease fire.

Khalil nodded his head gesturing to the Muezzin who stood and announced the second call to prayer. Sandi was distracted throughout the entire prayer. The moment it was finished and everyone dispersed, he tried to catch up with Omar for a better understanding of what was happening.

Two trucks approached from the south main road that stole everyone's attention. The men all maintained their relaxed postures as if they expected these visitors, but yet they fell silent with anticipation. Sandi turned to Omar with a questioning look.

"In one truck is his brother." Omar answered gesturing towards Khalil who was making his way to the road. "In the other you will find safe passage to the airport."

"And why am I going to the airport?" Sandi asked abruptly.

"Khalil believes it is best for your cause and ours."

Sandi looked upon Omar with bewilderment. "And when did we come to our fork in the road?" Sandi asked then spun off without waiting for an answer. "Khalil!" Sandi shouted. Already having an idea why Sandi was calling him Khalil left his brother and met Sandi halfway.

"Since Omar is speaking your words, it is to you whom I shall speak." Khalil looked over Sandi's shoulder at Omar then gave Sandi a nod of the head. "Then speak." Khalil instructed in a calm gentle understanding tone which only frustrated Sandi more. Sandi made his case to Khalil. Though Khalil already knew what Sandi was going to say he did the best thing he could for the moment, just listen.

"By God you are entitled to retribution, but you don't have to receive it here." Khalil said as he waved his hand then two groups of men stood. "I understand you have come thousands of miles, but you have come to where your enemy is the strongest." Khalil explained.

"The purpose of this occupation is to establish dominance of oil and to set up their war machine here in the east. Let us take a ride, if I don't make my point before we reach our destination you are welcomed to stay?"

"All praise is due to Allah." Sandi proclaimed because there was nothing Khalil could show him that would make him change his mind. Sandi climbed into the truck with Khalil who instructed the driver to pass by the Sheppard's base.

Sheppard is a multimillion dollar private security agency. Their sole purpose in Iraq is to provide security to contractors of special interest groups like the billion dollar American corporations that sent them there.

Their number one employer was Cortex a billion dollar international oil conglomerate. Of all the security agencies in Iraq and there were a few, Sheppard was the largest with mercenaries from around the world, working around the world.

They drove thirteen miles south to a scarcely populated area used primarily by Sheppard. The Sheppard's building stood twelve stories high and was surrounded by smaller buildings used for training, supplies, lodgings and reconnaissance. This complex was complete and self sustaining, it had to be practically stationed in the middle of a desert on hostile turf.

There were over a hundred and fifteen thousand private security employees in Iraq. Most of which were mercenaries or ex military. 49,000 of them worked for Sheppard and they all enjoyed complete impunity. "In other words they could shoot you on sight Sandi and get a bonus for it," Khalil teased.

That was easy for Sandi to imagine the way news reported shootings of disgruntle Iraqis like targets. Suddenly the 140,000 troops throughout Iraq seemed harmless by comparison.

**TERRORIST IN BROOKLYN**

Of course the new Cortex oil complex that was being constructed was only a few miles from the Sheppard's complex. From the set up Cortex had, it was impossible to attack them even with the help of Khalil.

Not only did Sandi loose the advantage he thought he would get being in his homeland, he lost heart. Khalil had Basir drive Sandi to the airport because Omar's or Uthman's presence would have given away Sandi's identity. On the way to the airport Sandi seen it with his own eyes, Cortexes new buildings under construction and almost complete.

## CHAPTER FIVE

**Special Agent Black got a phone call** from FBI field coordinator and he wanted some answers. Every answer SAB gave was the wrong one for the obvious reasons, he didn't have Sandi or have a clue where he was.

In less than a week three of Cortex buildings were demolished in New York. Since Cortex was a multibillion dollar conglomerate that funded and supported the Borish family and all their electoral pursuits, naturally when Cortex had a problem, a call to Senator Borish would usually be enough to get things done.

A call to President Borish himself would guarantee results, hence the call from Washington. The FBI field coordinator instructed Agent Black to go see Mr. Dercole who was in charge of Cortex Enterprises security and he was to give him his full cooperation. Not even two minutes after SAB got off the phone with the FBI coordinator there was a call from the lobby, he took it over the intercom.

"There is a Mr. Dercole and company to see you from Cortex Enterprise."

Agents McCarthy and Brinsky stopped what they were doing and gave SAB a look. "Thank you. Have them escorted to G3 conference room." SAB instructed then returned gazes with McCarthy and Brinsky. "Since you two are so interested, let's find out what's really going on."

McCarthy got up and led the way. From first sight as soon as SAB entered the conference room he knew which man was Mr. Dercole from the way his European features stood out as he glanced casually out the window.

One man was sitting to his right on a cell phone dispatching information. The third man was standing a little off from Dercole's left as if he was waiting for something. Neither of men moved as Mr. Dercole went to greet SAB.

"Special Agent Christopher Black, I thank you for taking this visit on such short notice," Dercole said as he made eye contact with SAB and extended his hand.

"Actually you saved me some gas money, I was just on my way to see you," SAB replied as he shook Mr. Dercole's hand and felt more than coldness. He passed over the feeling without giving it any thought and invited him to sit.

As soon as Mr. Dercole sat, the man that was on the phone stopped talking long enough to slide a folder down the long oak table. Dercole grabbed the folder that stopped in front of him. He opened it and spun it around for SAB to see its contents.

The first page was a complete profile on Iqbal Idris Sandi from the last job he had here in the states to the first job as a student in England as an apprentice to a chemical engineer. A listing of his family, friends and co workers in Iraq, England and the United States as well as the last time he spoke to each of them.

SAB wasn't impressed, but this was more than information you could gather off of someone's social security number. Sandi's name popped up the day before yesterday and from this Intel more and more the relationship between Sandi and Cortex seemed to have more of a commitment then Cortex admitted to.

SAB handed McCarthy the profile and sat quietly, he needed his moment to think. He had a lot of questions, like the one about the Arab who came to America for a slice of American pie. He gets it and out of the blue decides to turn his chem lab into a bomb factory. What was he part of, a sleeper cell that got a wakeup call and his target was Cortex?

"Ugh" "ugh" Dercole cleared his throat to snap SAB out of his daze. "Okay Agent Black, this is where you start asking questions."

That would be true if there was a chance SAB thought he could get Dercole to tell him about what was really going on with Cortex and why it was a terrorist magnet all of a sudden.

Before Mr. Dercole and company arrived SAB and Agent Brinsky put together a profile of their own, but of Cortex. They discovered Cortex wasn't just having problems with their New York offices. Pennsylvania, Texas and Florida were under attack and for some reason, Mr. Filler at the Trocoby Building or anyone else for that matter failed to mention it.

"Ask questions, that game of charades we don't have time to play," SAB stated in a stern voice. "One minute after I get off the phone with the head of the FBI Field Opts telling me it's time to earn my stripes you're standing in my doorway. I am sure you're not here to answer my questions. What can we do for Cortex or should I say Mr. Richard Calton?"

Mr. Dercole gave a nod of the head. "I was told you weren't much for wasting time," Dercole said and Mr. Telephone man stood and handed SAB a second folder.

Mr. Dercole and his associates both watched SAB's facial expression as he fingered through the file. Not able to read SAB's poker face Mr. Dercole began to explain to SAB what he was looking at as if his explanation would alter any thought SAB could conceive on his own.

"The men in the photos are Sahabah's of Jalal and Iqbal Sandi." Dercole began then went into telling him what this word Sahabah meant. He included its religious significance as he did when speaking to most Americans who he thought were culturally illiterate. He gave them the short version, that Sahabah meant companion, but its religious significance bounded them closer in life and death then whatever cause they took on.

"We have been dealing with this type for some time know and come to learn their ways." Mr. Dercole boasted and the man who stood aloof to Mr. Dercole's left stepped up. "Let him tag along, follow your lead. But there are times when he'll get on the moment indispensable information. We call it for the moment because it is only for the moment we have a Most Wanted tracked and boxed in. Since O' Patrick already knows our set up, you may have to follow his lead."

After Mr. Dercole departed, SAB had McCarthy introduce O' Patrick to the rest of the team. That was Agent Brinsky's cue to grab the folders and get the car. SAB and Agent Brinsky were going to pay a surprise visit to Mr. Filler at the Trocoby Building and he didn't see them coming.

He was on his way out to make a run. It was Agent Brinsky who spotted him as they were going through the revolving door. She was coming into the building and he was leaving, that was until she jammed her foot into the revolving door trapping Mr. Filler.

"Oops!" she said as Mr. Filler came to an abrupt stop colliding into the glass petition. Mr. Filler panicked and became frantic not knowing what was going on, until he seen Agents Black and Brinsky. Filler tried to conjure up a prior more traumatic experience to down play why he panicked and over reacted.

All the while SAB led the way towards Fillervision as Agent Brinsky entertained Mr. Filler's story of post traumatic revolving door drama. Once they stopped in front of Fillervision, Mr. Filler realized they did not come to hear his story.

"Got a little carried away ha? What can I do for my favorite FBI people?"

"We need a play back of the old footage of the Lynstone Building you showed us a couple of days ago," SAB instructed. Mr. Filler hit a switch and the last thing he was working on appeared on the mega screen.

There was Sandi talking to a man. He was about Sandi's build, a little darker in complexion, no facial hair and a fade. When Sandi turned away from the man to reach into a blue Benz SAB realized the place they were in was a parking lot. "Isn't that the footage from the latest explosion that you sent our office yesterday that's all over the news?" Agent Brinsky asked looking baffled.

"That's what it is," Filler replied without hesitation.

"Then who's the black guy he's talking to, we never were sent anything on him."

"Actually we don't know who he is," Filler replied as he removed the images and replaced them with the ones from the Lynstone Building they came to see. "We have been trying to figure out who he is but from that one shot feed it could be a conspirator or somebody he bumped into. Where did you want me to start this at?" Mr. Filler asked changing the subject.

SAB had him start from 6 AM when the doors opened, then he and Brinsky looked intensely from the time everyone entered the building until the time everyone left. They used face recognition software and they looked at all the surrounding surveillance and none of the men in the photos Mr. Dercole gave them was there, just Jalal and Iqbal Sandi.

"How about the footage from the second explosion, did you come up with anything yet?" SAB asked.

"Nothing. The blast destroyed everything useful."

"Why do I feel that was a complete waste of time?" Agent Brinsky asked after leaving Mr. Filler's office.

"Maybe because you're asking questions about things you suppose to be ignoring. When Dercole said he would call us after tracking down and boxing in a bad guy I didn't ask him why call us at that point?"

"Yeah I was curious about that also." Brinsky chimed in and SAB gave her a look. "Please tell me how you come from riding the little yellow bus to school to becoming an FBI agent. You must have family in high places!"

"Oh my, is that a joke Special Agent Black. I thought you were incapable of such things," Agent Brinsky said then leaned in and whispered. "What's the special occasion, you figured out something?" SAB smirked and looked at Agent Brinsky who thought she had him figured out, and gave her a wink. "Too soon to tell, let's take a ride."

SAB headed towards the Winston Building, the second building bombed that Mr. Filler said all the surveillance footage was destroyed. SAB found that odd since Cortex had access to the city monitoring surveillance system that would have caught something before and after at the very least. It was that same system they used to locate Sandi's truck and get a license plate number after the explosion at the Lynstone Building.

SAB parked across the street from the Winston Building. Minus the fire trucks, police cars and debris that was previously cleaned up, the building looked normal with the exception of the parking garage. From the outside the damage looked cosmetic, broken windows and slight structural damage, the inside on the other hand was hollowed out from the explosion.

SAB and Brinsky crossed over and stood in front of the Winston Building and looked up and down the block then across the street to see if any surveillance cameras were looking their way. Brinsky pointed across the street to a bank.

"I'll start over there."

While she went into the bank SAB strolled to the corner of the block looked up and was in direct view of the city street surveillance cameras. '*How could Fillervision not get this when the electrical power went unfazed by the blast?*' SAB asked himself.

"SAB come in." came across the radio as he made his way back up the block to the Winston Building. "Yes I'm listening," He replied.

"We have a situation in the lower level of the bank."

"Define situation?"

"I am watching a robbery in progress from the banks upper level surveillance."

SAB looked across the street at the bank and watched as a woman went into the bank. Before she could turn around and leave a set of hands reached out and grabbed her, that's all SAB could see from where he stood. He took a few steps to reposition himself. "I see a white male gray slacks, blue shirt how many other perps visible?"

"No other perps visible," Brinsky confirmed.

SAB told her he was going to be the next customer. Brinsky canvassed the bank from where she stood to see if she could get to the main floor without being seen. SAB walked across the street and tossed his radio in the car and casually strolled into the bank. Before he knew it he was thrown into a pile of customers.

SAB jumped up to his feet ready to go ballistic, "What the hell is going on?" he screamed. At the sight of a gun shoved in his face SAB took a step back.

"Take it easy brother, just making a quick withdrawal don't make this a hate crime."

"Click. Don't make this a justifiable homicide, now real slow," Agent Brinsky instructed as she reached for his gun and grabbed the barrel.

"Okay lady cop let the guns go or I'll blow it." Another man warned as he stepped away from the crowd that concealed him.

Everyone around him including SAB jumped back when the guy pulled out a bomb. "Aright, alright." Brinsky conceded as she managed to pull the gun out of the first perps hand. "I'm going to toss them so we can all walk out of here in one piece."

As soon as she was about to toss the guns a flat foot rushed in gun drawn and pointing at Brinsky. "Oh shit, i'm going to blow this motherfucker up!" the second perp with the bomb yelled in panic.

Before Brinsky could look at Special Agent Black all she heard was "POP" SAB let off a single shot. The bullet went into the forehead and out the back of the head of the second perp and the bomb was air bound. Agent Brinsky dropped the guns and flew.

SAB turned his gun on the cop, "FBI, she's FBI." Then he turned his gun onto the first perp who was reaching for his gun that Brinsky dropped. The perp froze and put his hands back in the air as a mob of police rushed into the bank.

SAB looked over at Brinsky who just laid there with the bomb she caught in her arms. "You suppose to dive away from the bomb, not towards it," SAB instructed shaking his head.

All the Rookie could do is shrug her shoulders and say "Touch down!" As she suspected the bomb was fake. She made her way back to the upper level surveillance area to get what they came for while SAB tried to wrap things up on the lower level.

The bank had footage from an ATM machine three hours prior to and after the explosion at the Winston Building. Though it was against policy to relinquish the tape to anyone without a court order, that was the least the bank could do for the agents, as long as it was returned quickly and discreetly.

That was no problem for SAB, his house was closer to the bank than headquarters. He could watch it at home and return it on the way back to headquarters. Agent Brinsky thought it was a good idea because it would give her a chance to see how he lived.

Agent Brinsky was impressed by his place, she didn't believe he lived alone. It was well decorated and the colors were coordinated with light earth tones as opposed to hard boy colors. While SAB prepared the video she looked around his place.

Is this your mother and father?" she asked. SAB stuck his head out of the room he was in and gazed at the agent with a look she didn't quite understand. She stared back at him, then repeated the question because all she could do at that point was assume he didn't hear her.

A smirk appeared on his face and his forehead crinkled as he struggled to answer her question. She took her eye off of SAB for a second to look at the picture again and when she looked back at SAB he was gone.

"SAB" Brinsky called out as she walked down the hallway towards the room he stuck his head out of. SAB stepped out of the room and Brinsky stopped in her tracks and looked into his eyes to see what was going on.

"Sorry about that, you caught me off guard with the question."

Brinsky glanced back at the portrait, "I only asked was that your mother and father."

"Yeah I know. Actually I heard you the first time and to answer your question, yes it is. Now come on the surveillance tape is playing."

Brinsky followed him into the room. The video was playing on a large plasma screen placed perfectly symmetrical to the mid size room that appeared to be used for entertaining purposes. The video showed the building in question and a small tunnel that led down into the parking lot used for the Winston Building and maybe a few others at best.

Agent Brinsky and SAB looked at each other as the unidentified man they saw on Mr. Fillers screen earlier that day emerge from the tunnel.

He pulled a cell phone out of his pocket, pressed a few buttons and began talking on the phone until a small havoc engineer company truck turned on to the sidewalk where he stood. The truck stopped long enough to flash a piece of paper at him. The black guy just glanced at his watch, said something to the guy in the truck and went back to talking on the phone.

Five minutes passed and nothing. SAB pressed fast forward until he seen the truck coming out of the tunnel. It didn't stop, the driver just waved and kept moving. SAB stopped the video, rewound it and played that part back in slow motion to get a better look at the driver. They couldn't tell if it was Sandi or one of his Sahabah, so he transferred the image to his computer to enhance it.

Even after enhancing the images they were unable to see the driver or passenger, but they were able to get a license plate number off the truck. SAB swung the key board around to Brinsky "Here, log in." she watched him through the corner of her eyes "And what's wrong with your password?" she asked with a smirk.

"The whole special agent thing, your classification goes under the radar."

"You know you really freaked me out with that little stare thing you did?"

SAB smiled, "Don't worry, I was just as freaked out as you were." He confessed then explained why. Since his mother died he nor his father has been any good on the topic. At least his father has had practice "on the topic" SAB kept saying, "her" instead of saying his mother or her name.

But SAB himself stayed away from the topic which was easy since he stayed away from family and spent all his time at work, where it was a professional courtesy not to pry in another's personal affairs. Brinsky's father was a bureaucrat and her mother specialized in brunches and being a politician's wife. Because they were alive and well and living in New Jersey, she didn't know what to say at that point. This was something she seen on Tyra or Oprah.

All this time she worked with him she was never able to get a glimpse of his personal life, but now she grazed and got a taste, it made no sense to turn back now. "She looked like a lovely woman, what happened?"

SAB gave her a look of reluctance but even the biggest inverts had to release sometimes. SAB took a deep breath and sighed with a shake of the head. "FBI, Federal Bureau of Investigation. I've been upgraded to special agent even and I-" SAB paused and regained eye contact with Brinsky who was hanging on every word.

"She was a translator for the United Nations. So from time to time she enjoyed traveling abroad, wherever the job sent her. But this time it was not work." SAB raised his hand tilting it back and forth to indicate maybe, maybe not, a half work half pleasure kind of thing.

"She was invited to a wedding of an old friend she did work for from time to time. My father and I refused to take a week off at such short notice, to a place we did not want to see anytime soon. My mother didn't care she was going that way regardless for a minor commitment." SAB smiled. "She said she was a celebrity out there. An African American woman who spoke two dialects of Arabic and she was so pious."

The smile evaporated from SAB's face. "There was an explosion at the wedding, a lot of people died and I never seen her again." SAB said abruptly wiping the smile off of Brinsky's face. "We never got closure because we never found her body and we still don't really know what happened out there. Now it's like me and my father are on different planets, we walk around with our heads in the clouds searching for our missing angel."

SAB glanced at the television, nothing not even the parking attendant. He looked back at Agent Brinsky, her eyes were heavy, her facial expression said she didn't take bad news well. He offered her something to drink and made his way to the kitchen while the video played out.

"SAB" "SAB" Brinsky shouted.

SAB rushed back into the room leaving the drinks behind. "What is it?" He asked looking at the screen and seeing nothing. Brinsky grabbed the remote then pointed it at the screen pressing rewind as she slowly pulled her hand back as if she was actually pulling the blue Benz out of the tunnel and onto the street with a magnet, then she pressed pause.

SAB didn't say anything, he just sat and waited for her to press play. The blue Benz stopped and turned on its turn signal as it waited in traffic, then dashed upon the sidewalk and into the parking lots tunnel.

There was no further need for suspense, she fast forwarded the video. Brinsky stopped when she seen Sandi leaving from the front entrance of the building, above the parking lot where he parked his car. He flagged down a cab tossed his brief case in and was gone.

SAB got up, went into the kitchen and came back with the two glasses he left on the counter. "Either you are real hospitable or you took that walk to the kitchen to buy enough time to figure out how that same blue Benz could be at two different explosions."

"What do you think?" SAB casually asked as he handed her a glass.

"I think you tried to steal a minute to figure it out."

"I meant about that?" SAB replied pointing at the screen with one hand and answering his phone with the other.

"O' Patrick got the call, they got one boxed in and he's waiting for you to say move out. Where are you?"

"On my way, but listen..." McCarthy watched O' Patrick as he listened into the phone. SAB's instructions were short, as soon as McCarthy got off the phone he told everyone they were going in, except Jenkins to whom he gave specific instructions.

The most wanted they had boxed in was Arif Salaam. According to his file he was responsible for one of Cortexes buildings in Newark, New Jersey and a proven agitator in Iraq. Agent Simms and Walton rode together while McCarthy stayed with O' Patrick.

O' Patrick was not the vocal type but he never passed up an opportunity to talk shop if he thought he could impress someone of legitimate rank. He told McCarthy he was a marine then signed on for the unlimited package with Cortex International Security. Unlimited power, paid privileges that came with the package on an international level.

Which meant, travel around the world and enjoy more jurisdiction than the local authorities in respective countries like Panama, Mexico, Iraq, South Africa, Afghanistan and other countries where Cortex had invested interest in resources and labor.

McCarthy was intrigued. He was a gold watch away from seeking new employment that offered these kind of benefits.

When they arrived it looked like McCarthy's crew was the first on scene. From the way Dercole described the most wanted as going to be boxed in or trapped McCarthy was expecting to see some muscle with high tech weaponry.

A Chevy Tahoe pulled in behind Agents Simms and Walton, four men poured out of it. McCarthy only recognized one of them and he was doing the same thing the last time he seen him, talking on the phone. Mr. Telephone man approached McCarthy and company leaving the other three men he came with by the Tahoe. Not seeing Special Agent Black Doyle gave O' Patrick a concerned look as he shook his hand.

O' Patrick gave one nod of the head, "Let's get this over with." He said firmly handing Doyle a blue wind breaker jacket with the big FBI letters on it. Doyle put it on then gave a command through his head set "Group one will standby, group two proceeding." Then Doyle gestured with his hand and one of the three men that he arrived with stepped up and laid out a blueprint across the top of the hood of McCarthy's car.

"You're going to need to know this."

McCarthy looked over the layout of the six story apartment building as Doyle pointed out the set up. Not even three minutes passed before a news truck pulled up. Simms nudged McCarthy, "Looks like you're going prime time." Once Doyle confirmed Arif Salaam was still in the building McCarthy didn't need to hear anymore, it was time to catch the bad guys.

McCarthy, Simms, Walton, O' Patrick, Doyle and one of Doyle's men took the steps up, the second of Doyle's men stayed down stairs positioning himself between the steps and the elevator. According to the information a family lived on the fourth floor in the apartment with Arif Salaam, which was confirmed when O' Patrick knocked on the door and a female answered.

She freely opened the door with a smile until she seen all the white faces with guns drawn. Instinctively her foot caught the door before it could open further, as if her foot would be an absolute barrier for these want to be intruders. "What do you want?" she fearlessly demanded as they glared at her as if looks alone could move her out the way.

"FBI" McCarthy shouted as he pushed the door along with the little woman behind it. O' Patrick and Doyle rushed into the apartment that was much larger than anticipated. It was two apartments in one. The two bedroom apartment turned out to be four. The only advantage was that the girl at the door didn't scream to warn those therein of the intrusion.

Doyle and O' Patrick took one side of the extended apartment, Simms and McCarthy covered the other side, while Walton and the extra hand covered the front door. There was no telling what they would find behind these closed doors and there was no time to think about it.

McCarthy and Simms secured as much of their side as quickly as they could. Pulling out the men or whatever bodies occupied these rooms, then pushed them up front to where Walton waited to secure them.

The adrenalin rush of going through a door not knowing what's on the other side was too severe for McCarthy. He long ago accepted the fact that he out lived his nine lives, but since he was filling in SAB's shoes he led first through the door as SAB would if he were there.

Most of the people they pulled out were women and children, there were only elderly men amongst them. Two shots rang out stopping McCarthy and Simms in their tracks. "Secure the area." McCarthy yelled down the hallway to Walton and then he took off in the direction he heard shots.

When McCarthy made it to the room where Doyle and O' Patrick were they had everything under control, placing cuffs on the last three men still alive while the other three lay dead. Special Agent Black and Agent Brinsky who were monitoring the activities as they approached were advised that two shots were fired, by the time they arrived it was over.

McCarthy briefed SAB as they walked through the apartment. SAB could picture McCarthy and Simms running down the narrow hallway to meet O' Patrick in the room giving cover, while Doyle cuffed the men.

"Three bodies?" SAB questioned after entering the room counting the dead. One of which was rolled almost in a fetal like position and the other two stretched out.

"A headline reading THREE DEAD TERRORIST will sound three times better than ONE DEAD TERRORIST." Doyle assured SAB.

"If headlines are what you're into." SAB reputed as he turned to leave.

## CHAPTER SIX

The Imam stood patiently by his car as he thought of the best way to handle this domestic situation. It wasn't the first time he heard about this African brother putting his hand on this Muslim sister. It was the first time he heard it from her.

Till today it was the Imams opinion that Sister Kayla and Daud got married primarily to secure citizenship for him. The going rate for that kind of thing varies anywhere from $8,000 to $15,000 respectfully depending on the arraignment. But any woman from Brooklyn would tell you, excessive handling is not part of the contract.

Usually under these circumstances when the Imam had to consult a married couple in dealing with an issue of this magnitude, he would make the brother move out until the matter was resolved and reconciliation made. Since the brother in question was African and lived on Fulton Street where a large percentage of his African brothers lived, kicking him out and leaving her there wouldn't help matters.

"Ya Imam, what's good." A man inquired as he crossed over to the Imam's side of the street. It took a few seconds for the Imam's eyes to regain focus as he returned from the daze he was in. The Imam smiled and extended his hand. "As Salaamu Alaikum Mujahid, longtime don't see. I thought you said you'd be coming by," The Imam questioned with raised eye brows.

"And I do come by here, I just walk on the other side of the street on way home from the halal meat market," Mujahid said gesturing in the direction from which he just came. Up the block there was a Muslim grocery store on the other side of the street next to the Halal meat market that he frequented regularly.

"Why are you standing by your car like you don't know if you want to come or go?" Mujahid asked.

"Actually I have to go, but I am trying to wait for my back up."

"Back up?"

"Yeah, I have a brother with hand problems and there's always the chance he could a little hostile amongst his homies."

Mujahid smiled. He hasn't seen Imam Ibraheem in awhile, so he figured this would be his opportunity to spend some time with the old timer without it having to be a religious experience. So to keep it that way when he got in route, Mujahid started talking about real estate and a house he was trying to get since the Imam was into real estate himself.

Mujahid went into his elaborate plot to kick some bums and drug dealers out of this vacant building he had his eye on and repair it while he squatted in it.

"You stand a better chance buying it from the city for close to nothing. Squatting has been outlawed some time ago. Is it city owned?" the Imam asked.

"More than likely." Mujahid replied with enthusiasm in his voice at the prospect the Imam would impart the secret to how he obtained two houses he commandeered from the city, that he uses to help the community. As they pulled up to their destination, the

Imam told Mujahid to give him a call later on that night. "I got a few numbers you could call."

"Yeah, I am sure you do!" Mujahid commented as he climbed out of the Imams old reliable Cadillac. The Imams eyes combed the street and stopped at the phone card store and taxi cab stand as they crossed the street dipping through the constant Fulton Street traffic.

"Daud" the Imam called out when he seen Daud walking down the street with two other brothers. All three men stopped and looked at the same time as if all three of their names were Daud.

Daud stepped away from the men he was with and greeted the Imam. "We are on our way to eat, would you like to join us?" Daud asked.

From his accent it wasn't hard for Mujahid to tell that Daud was Nigerian. He stood there fully garbed in his Ahkbaru, a three piece garment that is equivalent to the top of the line European business suit, only more colorful, a finer cloth with remarkable stitched embroidery.

The Imam was as forceful as a man five feet five inches could be as he declined the invitation and insisted that Daud give him a few minutes of his time to address a pressing matter. Mujahid watched curiously to see how long it would take before the Imam became impatient and demanded that Daud came with him.

Most brothers in the community took the Imam for granted mainly because of his size and the fact he never tried to compensate with a belligerent bark. Despite how humble the guy who led them in prayer seemed Mujahid knew personally there was another side of the little man that Daud nor his two African buddies wanted to experience.

Daud turned to his associates, "If I go and speak with him quickly I can-" Daud said in broken English then stopped mid sentence as if he forgot what he was about to say. His eyes were transfixed on a navy blue qimal. They all turned to see what he was staring at. The navy blue head wrap was all that could be seen with the large SUV blocking the rest of her, but Daud was sure it was Kayla.

Her eyes locked in on him as she crossed Fulton Street. Mujahid looked to the Imam for a confirmation, "The wife?" he asked. The Imam replied with a short nod of the head as he translated the stride in her step to mean something more than she was excited to see them. In fact she paid the Imam no mind as she shot past him, two Africans and Mujahid.

Before the Imam could be grateful he didn't have to go looking for her, Kayla quickly erased that thought from his mind "POW" Kayla slapped Daud so hard his African friends felt it because one of them subconsciously placed his hand on his face.

Of course it happened so quick it was unexpected, as was the flurry of punches that followed from the 6'1" muscular fellow that was trailing behind her since she left his house.

Mujahid could almost say he seen that coming with the exception he didn't know the woman heading their way with full steam with a guy in tow was coming to handle the same problem he and the Imam set out to handle, only a little more diplomatically.

Daud was shaken by the slap so the flurry of punches had him on his knees confused, trying to figure what just happened. His African comrades took a step backward and watched like passing spectators. The young fellow who was later identified as Kayla's brother fresh out of prison went to finish off Daud.

By then the Imam was already standing between Daud and Kayla's avenger. "I think he got the message," The Imam said trying to slow the young man down. Kayla's brother went to pass the Imam but paused for a moment and lifted his shirt to brandish a brand new shinny revolver. "Now do you get the message?" The young fellow menaced.

The Imam who was only a foot away from him quickly smiled and thanked the young man as he stuck his hand in the young man's belt and removed the firearm without blinking an eye. "How about you take a step back and we start all over." The Imam suggested as he stood with the gun holding it back at his waist pointing it at Kayla's brother.

"Please!" The Imam added to defuse the situation as the young man stood there slightly shook in seeing how easily he was disarmed. By now a crowd of spectators amassed, and amongst them were two uniformed cops fastly approaching.

"Now you see it." Mujahid said as he passed the Imam. "And now you don't." The Imam said as he finished the statement while rubbing his empty hands together.

"It's gone." One man said like he was watching a magic trick.

Mujahid took Kayla by the wrist, than gave Daud an instructive look to follow him as he turned and walked the opposite direction of the police.

The police didn't have a clue what was going on, they seen a crowd forming and heard something about a fight as they got closer. They watched as everyone dispersed then looked at each other and shrugged their shoulders and continued on their beat. Now there was no need for the Imam to step up and give his version of what happened. He went back to his car and headed back to the Mosque.

Before Imam Ibraheem could put his car in park Mujahid was opening the car door to let him out. "So what the boys in blue had to say?"

"No harm no foul."

"Yeah well, that's pretty much how Daud feels about the young buck putting the beats on him." Mujahid explained as he followed the Imam into the Mosque and began to remove his shoes.

"It's getting late, I got it from here." Imam Ibraheem said.

Mujahid smiled, "I was hoping you said that, here." Mujahid stuck his hand in his pocket and pulled out a .38 revolver. "The young brother asked about it and he's Muslim, took his Shahadah in prison."

"Thanks for the ride along. Will I see you on this side of the street sometime soon?" the Imam asked sarcastically already knowing the answer.

"Domestic squabbles, fights, guns, almost a police chase even!"

The Imam laughed at Mujahid's expressions. "Alright then at least give me a call and get the information for that building you are trying to get."

"Will do." Mujahid agreed.

## CHAPTER SEVEN

**To cut or not to cut, that was the question**. Cut his hair and beard to change his appearance or maintain his distinctive Professor look. Sandi had to go with what worked for him already.

The reservationist took Professor Steven Whitherpool's passport, looked at the photo then at the passport holder. She saw the face on the passport who was an American, Sandi was not in the equation.

Once he made it to his seat undetected, his only concern was what was going to happen when he landed at La Guardia. Ear hustling he overheard two passengers say something about being fingerprinted upon exiting the plane. He wanted to confirm what he heard but that would have only drawn attention to himself and his fears.

No sooner than exiting his flight he seen a big sign instructing all foreigners entering the United States to do a thumb print recognition. Suddenly Sandi's long strides shortened as the inevitable waited ahead. The American passengers veered to the right with passports in hand and foreigners entering the State veered to the left.

His eyes wandered hysterically for another option or alternate exit. As he neared his avoidable destination he could see the people zipping pass him in the mirror like reflection of the airports large glass windows.

For the first time he viewed himself from head to toe his baseball cap, button up shirt, jeans and track sneakers. Sandi still looked like Sandi, the Arab American who lived in America for the better portion of his life.

Sandi pulled Whitherpool's passport out and veered to the right. He flashed his passport in the same nonchalant manner the people in front of him did and kept walking. The walk through the remainder of the airport seemed like forever. As soon as he hit the pavement he wanted to drop to the ground and kiss it, instead he jumped into the first cab he seen.

Sandi didn't bother looking at the driver, he didn't want to make eye contact. Instead he glanced at the man's identification posted on the meter, he was an African American. Sandi quickly slid behind the driver and pulled his baseball cap over his eyes and looked out the window so the driver couldn't see his face.

"What's it going to be boss?" The driver asked as he glanced back at Sandi through his rear view mirror.

That was a good question. Sandi didn't give it much thought since he never thought he would make it that far. He leaned forward shoved his hand in his pocket and came out with $40 and handed it to the driver "Hold on to this while I try to remember the address, just take it slow."

"You see the traffic, slow is the only way. Can I get a borough?"

"Sure, Manhattan."

As the driver reached back to take the money Sandi read the faded writing on the man's tee-shirt. "You Muslim?" Sandi asked.

"Na, why you ask me that?"

"Your tee-shirt says Mecca!"

"Ah man this old ass shirt. Harlem man, the Mecca of the world."

"I don't understand," Sandi said.

"Don't worry about it man, like I said it's an old ass shirt."

Sandi heard the bitterness in the taxi driver's voice which made him more curious because he made it sound like Mecca didn't exist anymore, so Sandi pried further. Before the driver answered anymore questions he took a better look at his passenger and realized he was an Arab.

"Back in the sixties Harlem was like the center of the world for the black man." The driver paused as if to give his statement some thought, then he snapped out of it. "I don't know, I think it was Malcolm X or one of those cats who called it Mecca. I guess it stuck. And slowly but surely between the high rent, unbelievable mortgages and taxes." The driver paused again this time he took another look at his passenger.

"Anyway a Muslim brother I know said if I can't live in Mecca to migrate to Medina, so I have been living in Brooklyn ever since."

The ride was quiet for a moment as the driver forced his way through the crawling traffic and Sandi related to the fact that going back to Manhattan wasn't such a great idea. Sandi slouched into his seat, readjusted his baseball cap for comfort and drifted into thought. The word migrate triggered a thought about the life of the Prophet of Islam. How he migrated from Mecca to Medina to escape the infidels.

"Hey listen man, forty bucks isn't going to go far in this traffic, you figured out that address?"

"Yeah, Medina." Sandi said with a smirk.

"I still need and address."

"4<sup>th</sup> Avenue and Atlantic."

*'I could definitely blend in here,'* Sandi thought as the cab came to a stop in front of the Mosque where Arabs and others stood around talking. Sandi thanked the driver and hopped out to stretched. He pulled his cap off his head and ran his fingers through his hair.

Sandi quickly put his cap back on his head when he seen two uniform officers standing a few feet inside the Mosque entrance talking to someone.

Sandi figured he could stall for a minute, take a walk up Atlantic Ave and look inside some Muslim stores. The second he was about to turn and walk he heard radio static and a transmission that came over a walkie talkie, suddenly his feet felt like fifty pound dumbbells.

He stood there stuck as two plain clothes cops passed him by. His heart started racing and suddenly he felt like he had to make a bowel movement. He couldn't just stand there. A crowd was amassing only a few feet away from him so he made his move and joined that crowd that was just getting off of one bus and transferring over to another.

"Hey Lisa." A guy yelled out from his car as he swerved to the curb. Lisa wasted no time, "Transfer anyone?"

Sandi was the closest to her. He grabbed it without hesitation. Lisa stepped off the curb, opened the door to the car and turned around and gave Sandi a look.

"Come on girl, we're in the bus stop and the bus is coming," The driver instructed.

Lisa jumped in, closed the door and her friend sped off. When the bus pulled in Sandi got on and rushed to the back of the bus and secured a seat in the corner by the window. He wiped the sweat off his brow then took a deep breath, than another, but the third one he held and let out real slow. It worked, he felt much calmer.

Calmer as in he didn't hear any police sirens or no one started pointing and screaming, call the police. But the fact remained he didn't have any money nor a clue as to where the bus was taking him, and he was starving.

His eyes combed the streets looking for a valid enough reason to abandon his only mode of transportation through Brooklyn. His sunset prayer came and gone and the streets were dark.

Finally, two woman with their heads wrapped caught his attention. Trailing behind them were a group of men, some with kufis on their heads some without. There had to be a Mosque nearby Sandi thought as he reached for the bell. He missed that stop but got off at the next one a little further up, so he had to work his way back, but to where?

Coming from the other direction was a Muslim woman. Sandi slowed down to see where she would go. She climbed some steps and entered a building that said Masjid. '*If she entered from there, the men must enter from down stairs*,' he reasoned.

He opened the gate to the yard and seen no movement so he assumed everyone was offering prayer. There was a curtain on the first floor window so he couldn't see inside. He took off his baseball cap placed it in the small of his back, than entered through the door that was partially open.

He crossed the threshold with his right foot and recited a small prayer for the occasion. He was met by the fragrance of burning incense and Quranic recitation that was coming from the upper level that was relaxing and also an indication that he was on the wrong floor.

The hallway light flickered on and off as if the bulb was weak. He tried to move between flashes of light to make his way to the staircase. As the light flashed a second time he saw someone ahead of him. The hallway went dark and the man disappeared, from behind him another man appeared. Sandi didn't know the man was there until the man moved close enough to whisper, "You make one move, I will kill you!"

After feeling a cold piece of metal on the back of his head Sandi stood quietly and awaited instructions. To the right of him he heard a sliding door open but no light came out of it. He was pushed in that direction then Sandi felt a second set of hands patting and frisking him.

The front of his button up shirt was ripped open. But this time after he was frisked he was swept off his feet, laid face down and he felt someone's knee crushing his baseball cap as they kneeled on his back to keep him down.

"Why are you here?" a voice calmly asked.

"To make prayer and seek food," Sandi answered then felt the gun again.

"Who are you and why are you here?" The voice asked again, but more firmly.

"By Allah I seek prayer and want to make food."

"You mix your lies. But before I kill you I will show you what you seek. The two of you can die together."

A light came on and another man laid right beside Sandi with a man in black holding a gun to his head. The man on the floor was Sandi's complexion and had a beard like his, only he was dressed differently like a Muslim. He had on a long garb with slacks under it.

All three men looked at each other, neither of them knew if they should believe him or not. The one holding his knee in Sandi's back questioned him again. Sandi didn't know what to say because he didn't know what was going on. Sandi asked to be told at least what he or this man next to him was accused of.

When they told Sandi that the man was accused of being an agent, placed in the Mosque to spy on the Muslims and spread dissidence, Sandi became brazen and began to wrestle his way from under the man's knee.

"My life and death is for the pleasure of Allah and you accuse me of this!" Sandi growled in anger for the first time.

A door in the back of the room swung open. Sandi stopped struggling long enough to look up. A tall bearded man walked in wearing a long garb, under it he wore jeans and had on a pair of Jordan sneakers. "Who is he?" The man asked.

"I don't know," The man with his knee in Sandi's back replied.

"Who does he say he is?"

"Muslim."

"Huh, I'm glad it's your foot on his neck, not mine. You searched him let him up."

Al Amin got off his back and put his gun in his belt as Sandi stood. The other man was still held face down to the floor with duct tape on his mouth, hands and feet. Sandi glanced at all four men in the room and they looked back at him. The tall bearded man walked over to Sandi and introduced himself.

"I am Hussein Ibn Abdullah." He pointed, "The guy right there who had his foot on your neck is Al Amin, he is Hassan and last but not least there is Idris." Hussein said pointing at the smallest guy in the room. "Now who might you be?"

Sandi hesitated for a moment. Nothing these brothers said indicated they were police or would turn him over to the police, actually to the contrary. In fact, Sandi considered he might even gain ground with them once they knew who he really was.

"Iqbal Idris Sandi!" He proclaimed then paused waiting to see if they knew of him. When no one said anything Sandi studied Hussein's face because he couldn't believe they haven't heard his name over the last week or so, or seen pictures of him plastered on the news and news papers.

Idris and Al Amin scooped up the man that laid on the floor gagged and bound and placed him on his feet. Hassan placed a gun to his head. Al Amin and Idris quickly took a step away from him to avoid any possible brain or blood on their garbs. The man began to plead but the gag covered his mouth so only incoherent sounds came out.

Hassan moved the gun from his head and turned to Sandi and placed it to his head. "Last chance, why are you here?"

Sandi swallowed hard and fear passed over him and anger appeared. "Ya yu hallathina aminu taqwa la," Sandi said making eye contact with Hassan after telling him if he believed in Allah he should have fear.

"Do you fear Allah Iqbal Idris Sandi?" Hassan retorted.

"Of course I do," Sandi quickly replied as if he was offended. Without anymore Hassan handed Sandi the gun. Sandi carefully took it as he watched Hassan then quickly glanced around the room at Hussein, Idris and Al Amin

"He is a government agent sent to destroy us. If you fear Allah place the gun to his head and pull the trigger," Hassan demanded.

"What proof do you have of this?"

"What proof we have you are not an agent?" Hassan retorted.

"I know what the problem is." Idris said speaking for the first time as he approached Sandi. He took the gun out of Sandi's hand and placed a silencer on it.

Idris slowly raised the gun to the agents head. Idris was the shortest in the room so he had to reach up, but not far because of the long barrel of the Desert Eagle with the silencer on it.

ANTHONY BREWER

Idris looked at Sandi. "How many people have you stood face to face with and decided you had the right to take their life?" Idris turned to the agent. "You already know who I am, so I will tell you why. Aside from the obvious since you are not Muslim you would not know. I have the right above everyone here because the Mosque in which you were caught spying is my fathers. I am Idris Ibn Ibraheem."

Idris pulled the trigger and turned to see Sandi's reaction. The slug from the Desert Eagle exited through the upper left side of the agents head. Al Amin snatched the hot shell casing from the slug out of the air. "You see he knows what he did and why he died. I know you can't say the same about all those people you blew up," Idris taunted.

Sandi gave Idris a sharp look as they all stared at him to see if he could offer a rebuttal. Sandi stood there speechless. Hussein, Hassan, Idris and Al Amin all knew about that last building that was blown up and attributed to Sandi. It enraged them all hearing of the news of close to a hundred people murdered in the explosion. It did not matter if they were Muslim or non Muslim, it was unacceptable. No one said another word they had to deal with the matter at hand, the dead agent.

# CHAPTER EIGHT

**Special Agent Black got off the phone with Mr. Dercole** who expressed his appreciation of the FBI's assistance in the apprehension of Arif Salaam. SAB also had to deal with the flip side of that.

Not only was the now deceased Arif Salaam an accomplished family man now dead, but so were the two other men killed in their home. Which brought on echo's of outcries from family, friends and colleagues of Arif Salaam.

These colleagues were journalist with access to news papers and the ears of the politicians and the public. SAB closed his office door and pulled his blinds because at the end of the day the Bureau would prevail and the headlines will read **"FBI RAIDED HOME OF KNOWN TERRORIST ARIF SALAAM, THREE TERRORIST DEAD."**

Despite its veracity it would quail the echo of outcries. No one wants the burden of an unpatriotic agitator at a time when America is at war with terrorism.

SAB's silence was broken by a gentle knock on the door. Agent Brinsky stuck her head in, "McCarthy is on with NYPD, they found a body that matches the description of Sandi."

*'That would be too easy,'* SAB thought as they made their way over the Brooklyn Bridge. But at the same time it would explain why Sandi hasn't been heard from in a more than a week.

## ANTHONY BREWER

The body was found in an abandoned park on the border of Bedstuy, Bushwick and East New York by a woman walking her dog. She called 911 and it was the first car on the scene that radioed in that the body found was Iqbal Idris Sandi.

The park was shabby and unkept, with grass almost a foot high growing through the pavement. It was obvious from the excrement this was where people curbed their dogs. You had to enter at your own risk.

"Was the identification confirmed?" SAB asked the detective who introduced himself as Homicide.

"Confirmed, I don't know how anyone could have made the identification in the first place, did you see the guy?"

SAB looked at the body that laid face down on the pavement with his body twisted, with a portion of his face missing. And if you looked carefully enough you could see something wedged under his twisted body.

"I wouldn't do that if I were you, the Sandi's have a way of blowing up when you move them the wrong way," O' Patrick warned as he moved in to take a glance at the body.

"You want to play it safe and wait for the bomb squad?" The detective asked as he stood, heedful of O' Patrick's warning. It was needless to say that SAB came prepared. Agent Walton stepped up carefully as if the dog droppings were land mines. "You all can watch me work or run for cover," He taunted as he maneuvered between the Homicide Detective and O' Patrick.

"I finally get the chance to see how the FBI work up close and personal," O' Patrick retorted sarcastically.

Walton took a hold of the corpse's wrist. His arm was out stretched in an odd kind of way. Walton raised it slowly with the intent to unfold the guy and see what was under him. **A beeping sound went off.** O' Patrick tensed and shifted his feet almost in panic, prepared to take flight.

"Oops gotta go." The Homicide Detective announced as he shut off the alarm on his watch and O' Patrick started breathing again.

"Special Agent Black, I try to keep it at eight hours a day to earn my pay." The detective turned and looked at the corpse, "If that's your man make sure my name goes up in the opening credits, I don't like to be left out. If it's just somebody someone didn't like and they put him where no one likes to go, pass him on to the cop who claimed he was Sandi and let him do the paper work."

SAB watched as the detective make his way around his colleagues, over the piles of excrement then lost him after he dipped through a hole in the fence. The park was quiet and no one else moved as Agent Walton slowly turned the corpse over revealing what was wedged beneath it, a news paper. In full view was the front page with a picture of Iqbal Idris Sandi on a MOST WANTED poster.

Agent Brinsky came up behind SAB and whispered into his ear. "We got action at Sandi's house." SAB looked at all the faces around him and located the officer who identified the corpse as Sandi.

"You could have saved us all a lot of time by coming clean." SAB scorned. The officer's face reddened with embarrassment.

"Walton, hang around as see if there is a connection," SAB instructed.

\*     \*     \*     \*     \*     \*     \*     \*     \*

Agent Brinsky pulled up to Sandi's house where FBI and NYPD were taking statements trying to get a grip on what just happened. Two FBI agents and two NYPD officers were handled, by whom it was not clear. SAB and Brinsky listened as one of the cops gave his account of what happened.

"My partner seen someone approaching about a half a block off and he gave me a nudge," The officer said gesturing with his elbow then continued his story as if the nudge was significant. "It looked like an old lady from how she was hunched over so we went back to talking. Not even moments later my left leg gives and there's an arm around my neck."

"He was out like a light." His partner chimed in. "And before I could draw my weapon he already dropped Tom and was full circle 'BANG', his foot was in my chest. I go flying and before I hit the ground he was on me." The cop who had to be in his twenties and physically fit looked away from Agent Brinsky as he made his last admission, "That was the last thing I saw."

"You said he?" Agent Brinsky asked shoving a photo in his face. "Is this the man?" The officer who was knocked out shook his head no. The other officer that was put to sleep just shrugged his shoulders. "I know this is not a pleasant experience for you boys but I need more of an effort with the description." Agent Brinsky pressed. SAB turned to Agent Brinsky gave her a nod and went into the house.

The agents who were inside of the house story were not much different. He felt a breeze, seen the little fat boy look then run off. Just as fast as the agent looked to see what the kid saw he was knocked unconscious.

His partner didn't see anything. She was up stairs looking around. When she came down stairs she found her partner stretched out on the floor and the kids were gone.

"At what point did you here gun fire?" SAB asked.

"On my way into the kitchen to make sure the children were not in there, and then I heard the barrage of shots. I drew my weapon and quickly rushed to the front. As soon as I opened the door there was an officer laying at the bottom of the steps and another one a little further away, I thought they were dead. And that's when I seen the van pulling off."

The agent went on to explain that at first impression of seeing the van she didn't know if it was civilian. It wasn't until see ran into the street to get the license plate number of the van did she see two men laying in the street, one in the middle of the street and the other laying in the gutter.

"From the way the men in the street were dressed I thought they were agents. I checked their pulses, they both were dead."

Special Agent Black didn't need to hear anymore. What he needed to do was put things in to perspective. The two suits lying in the street belonged to Mr. Dercole of Cortex International. Apparently they were sitting around waiting for the same reason the FBI were, hoping that Sandi or one of his protégés showed up to check on his niece and nephew.

They showed up alright. This extraction clearly demonstrated that Sandi was alive and well, and he had help. By the looks of the mercenaries lying in street, he had good help.

At this point it was clear that everyone involved had their own agenda so it was time for Special Agent Black to take off the tap shoes and little white gloves and get an agenda of his own. But in retrospect he was missing some essential pieces of the puzzle, he was just going to have to improvise.

Getting a description from the two officers that were attacked on the streets was like pulling teeth, but it was worth it. The perp according to their combined efforts was around 5'6", 170 lbs, light skinned African American with black hair and brown eyes. They also said, "He was fast as hell." End of quote.

The description given by the FBI agent of the man driving the van confirmed that Sandi's protégés were African American. That coupled with the body found in the park, all signs pointed back across the Brooklyn Bridge, but before SAB went back that way there a few things he had to take care of.

SAB's first course of action was to brief his team and get everyone on the same page. From SAB's first meeting with Cortexes Mr. Dercole he realized Cortex was not being forthcoming, so it was only natural to sit on the bits and pieces of intrinsic information and wait for his chance to parley.

## TERRORIST IN BROOKLYN

As it related to Arif Salaam; McCarthy, Simms, Brinsky nor Walton knew he was assassinated. Jenkins had the visual and McCarthy and Simms the audio.

When McCarthy called SAB telling him O' Patrick got the call saying they had a most wanted boxed in, SAB didn't want his team walking into something unexpected so he sent Jenkins ahead to be their eye in the sky with his sniper rifle.

Jenkins positioned himself better than expected in the building across the street from the targets. Unable to view the entire apartment Jenkins focused on the best view he had, six men of Arab decent in one room.

It looked as if they were praying because they were bowing and prostrating. The men didn't see when Doyle came from behind putting a silencer to Arif's head and pulling the trigger. It was at that very moment the two men tried to come to Arifs aid that they were shot dead by O' Patrick, hence the two shots McCarthy and Simms heard.

"I get three bodies dropped on me in less than an hour and now all of a sudden all of our suspects are African American." SAB waved a photo of the man they got from the bank surveillance who appeared to be the parking attendant. SAB slammed the photo onto the conference table, "This is the catch of the day." SAB paused but only long enough to find the snap shot of the two dead suits killed by Sandi's house, "And while we are looking at photos I have this one for you."

ANTHONY BREWER

Everyone glanced at the photo. McCarthy stared the longest. The photo answered a question in the back of his mind about risk versus reward for the international cops O' Patrick bragged about.

"Just to give you guys an idea what we're up against besides the bomber. What's worse than mercenaries? That's right, the people that killed them so let's be careful out there."

O' Patrick was not invited to this little meeting, he had trouble with clearance. He might not have gotten there to hear what he wanted to but conveniently he did get clearance in time to get an earful of what SAB had set up for him, he actually came on time.

As O' Patrick entered the conference room SAB took a hard stare at his watch then a O' Patrick, "Can we start now?" SAB asked. "By all means," O' Patrick replied as he flopped into the closest seat to him.

"Take one and pass it around." SAB instructed. As the stack of photos reached O' Patrick SAB watched for a reaction, there was none. The photo was of the parking attendant seen with Sandi before the explosion. SAB didn't know who this man was, his relationship to Sandi nor why Cortex was hiding his very existence, but he was going to find out.

As soon as everyone departed O' Patrick sat in his car and called Dercole. "They got a picture of Smith, they think he is one of Sandi's crew," O' Patrick explained.

"Good, they know nothing let's keep it that way. You know where his family is, kill his mother, father, dog it doesn't matter, but you better find him first. I'll have Doyle meet you in Brooklyn at the Smith's."

Agent Brinsky turned to SAB with a pale look on her face after listening to Mr. Dercole cold bellicose tone. She got more than she bargained for from the bug she placed in his car. "Is it safe to say I am glad we are on his side of these guys?"

"Well let's enjoy our safety net before it expires and go get something to eat. We have a date with a journalist that has something to say that's not fit for print."

Agent Brinsky suspiciously looked at SAB from the corner of her eye, she quickly changed from a pale white to a rosy pink. "I was with you all day, when did you get a call?"

SAB observed the look on Brinsky's face, "Why are you looking at me like that?" SAB asked.

"Don't mind me, continue." Brinsky instructed.

"She said she knows who we are dealing with so it was safe to assume that our phones are tapped and we're being followed so this arrived earlier." SAB reached into his pocket, pulled out an envelope and handed it to Brinsky. She snatched the envelope, pulled out the letter and began to read it. She only took her eyes off the letter long enough to glance at SAB to give him a nod of approval.

"How do you know it's a journalist?" Brinsky asked. Not seeing the timing between the death of Arif Salaam, the tone of all the outcries over his death and the journalist being the most outspoken and ignored. The real question of the day was what did this journalist have to say that was not fit for print.

While Special Agents Black and Brinsky were heading out to dinner with the journalist. Agents McCarthy and Simms were to follow O' Patrick to the Smith's house so they could find out who Smith was and why Cortex didn't want anybody to know about him.

As expected it was Agents Jenkins and Walton who got the first taste of action for the night. Their task was to clear the way for SAB and Brinsky to attend their evening engagement unmolested by Cortexes men.

As soon as Brinksy pulled into the street she could look in her rear view mirror about five cars back and see a blue sedan also pulling out. She turned left the sedan turned left. She turned right and slowed down, the sedan turned right and slowed down.

Then a black SUV pulled behind the sedan with flashing lights in the headlight, Agents Jenkins and Walton jumped out.

It started as a license and registration check, but since the mercenaries didn't appreciate getting pulled over showed they some attitude. Jenkins and Walton had to remind them that intimidation didn't work with the FBI. They disarmed them called the NYPD and had locals run their papers for the nice shinny firearms they were carrying, which took all night.

Before SAB went into the restaurant he checked up on Jenkins and Walton. Jenkins told SAB the guys they pulled over were not Cortexes men, their permits said they were Shappards. SAB didn't quite know what that meant, but he knew they would not be joining them for dinner.

The letter said reservations were under the name Pandora. Brinsky and SAB were escorted to a table in the far rear of the restaurant where a woman patiently sat and waited as she enjoyed her aperitif. She stood as the agents approached and cheerfully greeted them by first names that weren't their own.

"Excuse me for that, in my business somebody is always listening and everyone is always watching, at least it's good to believe it." She explained.

No sooner than they sat and picked up a menu a waiter appeared, Pandora ordered than dismissed him. "I am not going to thank you'll for coming because there is a chance I might regret this in the long run." She began.

"Then why do it?" SAB asked.

"The same reason you and this young lady protect the land and the people on it, it's your job. I am a journalist my job is to inform those people you protect." The journalist made eye contact with SAB, "You can almost say I protect people by giving them vital information."

SAB gave her a quizzical look then sat back in his seat and waited for her to dispense this vital information. Agent Brinsky seen that probing look SAB had on his face, despite it he remained silent so she did the same. They did come there to hear what she had to say, once Pandora seen she had their attention she began.

"I am a Noble Laureate in my field so I have no qualms bringing the people what they need to know. My problem is when they start to shoot the messenger."

"I don't understand, if you have problems exercising your first amendment rights why all the cloak and dagger routine?" Agent Brinsky asked with a look of disappointment.

ANTHONY BREWER

"Were you one of the agents who shot down Arif Salaam in cold blood?" The journalist asked Brinsky in a confrontational manner.

"You already know the answer to that so stop footing around. The real question is, are you on Cortexes list of bad people they want out the way?" SAB asked, again with the probing look.

The very mention of being on Cortexes list made the journalist look around the restaurant then at a table where two men sat.

"No," She replied firmly then looked at both agents to see if they knew otherwise. "Arif Salaam was a journalist, that's my headline." She stated in a fit of frustration. "I felt it was my duty to tell someone, so I am telling you Special Agent Black because it serves my greater purpose."

Pandora took a swig of her drink then turned to Agent Brinsky, "And yes young lady I know Cortex killed Arif and he was no terrorist. Blowing someone up with the truth is just good reporting or keeping it real as my daughter calls it." She stopped and took another swig.

"That's the problem Arif was too real, so real he signed his own death warrant. He wrote a lot of stories on how the U.S. took Iraq for oil. So what right everyone knew that." The journalist laughed to herself like it was an inside joke and just like that her smile vanished, then she sighed.

"An article came out from one of those leftist grass root groups calling journalist parakeets. Reporter's just telling stories already reported, that didn't help Arif's conscious. It was already bothering him that he was not reporting what was really going on in Iraq. I'm not talking about the fluff you hear about on network news.

So Arif does the story 'Iraq is invaded by terrorist.', then he follows up with 'Invading a country near you.' Insisting that the U.S. was setting up in Iraq in preparation for Iran or whatever Middle Eastern country they could justify going to war with.

"I can't see how Arif reporting what's been said for the past eight years got him killed now. I think you got us here and got cold feet so I'm going to have to go with Agent Brinsky's assessment, if you or Arif had problems exercising your first amendment rights-"

"Stop saying that!" she shouted losing her composure for the first time. "There are no first amendment rights in Iraq. Over 333 journalist have been killed in Iraq since the war and all major news networks bombed by U.S. missile attacks."

She sat back in her chair with a renewed calmness. "I left Iraq a long time ago to escape persecution, and if that was not enough." She gestured with her head towards the two men who were watching her and anyone coming her way. "If all that fails, I have you." She said as she reached across the table and placed her hands on top of SAB's.

"I summoned you here, to provide you with information to help your investigation along against Cortex. Because God forbid, something happens to me I want you primed and ready."

She reached into her bag, pulled out a manila envelope and placed it on the seat between her and SAB. "Take it when you leave."

SAB's cell phone rung, he listened into it and asked one question "Where?" then he hung up then refocused his attention to

Pandora. "What do you mean primed and ready, for what?" SAB inquired only to be brushed off with a dismissive glance.

SAB seen he wasn't getting anywhere with this so he gave Agent Brinsky, who was already standing in her seat, the it's time to go look. The journalist placed her hand on top of SAB's to try and stop him from leaving.

"I have all the information you need, it's just too soon to give it to you but I will give one thing that will help in the end game, but only if you understand this now. Why does the Cortex one of the most powerful industries in the world even bother with the FBI?"

She didn't bother waiting for SAB to reply. "It's politics, in Iraq they could do what they want, even kill with impunity. In the U.S. their hands are tied their just another business with a lot of money."

"Unless they got you, the FBI to give you names and faces like Arif Salaam for you to post on America's Most Wanted list. Now the same terrorist that killed in Iraq with impunity, are now in Brooklyn with your help of course, still killing with impunity."

The journalist looked at Agent Brinsky "I asked you when you first came to this table did you kill Arif Salaam and you were indignant about it. What would you think now if I asked the same question. Instead, I'll just ask you who are the real terrorist?"

Pandora thanked the agents for coming, than whispered in SAB's ear. "I can answer all your questions that will change this case and your life but you have to wait for me, it will be worth the wait."

## CHAPTER NINE

**The last and only address of George Smith** belonged to his parents Jennifer and Ronald Smith. His mother Jennifer Smith worked as a phone operator at TCI for the last seven years. She got off of work at 11 PM and her husband who worked for the Department of Corrections got off at eleven also and was only a few minutes away which explained why she had her own personal chauffeur.

He would drive her to and from work with the exception of the nights like tonight when his old unreliable truck conked out on him and Mrs. Smith had to catch a ride with a coworker.

The Smith's home was a two story one family abode, so it was safe to assume that the middle aged woman that climbed out of the jeep and went into the Smith's home was George's mother. After sitting and waiting for three hours, Doyle and O' Patrick saw no reason to wait any longer. As soon as the jeep pulled off they made their move.

When the door bell rang Mrs. Smith only had two steps left to reach the top, she was not about to go all the way back down those steps without discarding her coat and purse. '*Who the hell is it this time of night?*' she thought as she dropped her stuff on her bed and made her way to the bedroom window that overlooked her front steps.

When she saw two white men in suits the first thought that came to mind was the police. She paused for a moment to try and imagine what they could want that late hour of the night. Without delay she yanked at the window and seen it was locked. All she could think about was how many times she told her husband not to lock the bedroom window.

From the jerking sound of the window O' Patrick and Doyle looked up and patiently waited for her to open the window. "Mrs. Smith?" Doyle asked.

"Yes, what seems to be the problem?" Ms. Smith asked. Doyle took a glance around, "This is a private matter, can you please come down?"

Mrs. Smith took her sweet time getting down stairs and when she finally did she asked them to show some identification. Doyle and O' Patrick looked at each other, Doyle pulled out his Cortex security clearance card.

"That doesn't say police." Mrs. Smith hollered through the door.

"No Mrs. Smith it says security. Your son George worked for us and we need to talk to you about where he might be." Doyle explained.

"Then you need to come back at a better hour when my husband is home."

"Mrs. Smith this is a matter of national security." O' Patrick insisted.

"It's my security I'm worried about. Plus I am so tired of talking, been doing it all day. Come back in the morning." She demanded as she turned her back and mumbled something about national security on her way to the kitchen.

## TERRORIST IN BROOKLYN

The clock on the wall read 11:45 as she pulled out the food she prepped before going to work earlier that day. She wrestled with the thought of calling her husband to see what was keeping him, but when she felt the breeze coming from the front door she was glad she didn't. Then she wished she did when Doyle and O' Patrick walked into her kitchen.

She didn't scream or panic. She calmly slid the dish of pasta into the microwave, then looked over her shoulder at her intruders while she punched numbers into the microwave key pad. "You know, my husband should be walking through that door any moment now."

"So why not answer one simple question and send us on our way without incident." Doyle suggested.

Mrs. Smith turned with a scornful look on her face. "You stand in my kitchen uninvited and say without incident!"

"Mrs. Smith, this is not one of those situations where one could say it couldn't get any worse. Because it could, now please, where is your son?" Doyle asked as he took a step towards her.

Mrs. Smith figured this would be a good time to stall with hopes her husband would walk through the door because she had no intentions on telling these men where her son was at, not knowing why they really wanted him.

"I have a number and address upstairs." She quickly replied as she opened the microwave and replaced one dish with another then invited them to sit while she retrieved the information. Of course they refused to sit and insisted on following her up stairs.

As soon as they made it to the bottom of the stair case the front door swung open, it was Mr. Smith. "I finally make it home and somebody is in my parking spot." Were his first words as he studied the two white men standing in the hallway with his wife, "What's going on here?" he asked after seeing a disturbed look on her face.

"They say they're looking for George," His wife replied and at the same time tried to walk towards her husband. O' Patrick grabbed her by her arm and Mr. Smith didn't know what to do so he pulled out his work pistol, but Doyle was faster. "Now put that down before someone gets hurt." Doyle instructed.

"Let go my wife first." Mr. Smith demanded. O' Patrick held her tighter as she tried to pull away.

"POW" Doyle shot Mr. Smith and Mrs. Smith let out a scream that could have waken the whole neighborhood.

"Now see that was really unnecessary." Doyle commented as he kicked Mr. Smith's gun away and grabbed him by the shoulder. "Now let's go up stairs. I believe there's an address and phone number up there for me."

Before they made it to the top of the steps the phone rang out, O' Patrick looked at Doyle. Doyle shook his head no.

"Like she said, she's tired of talking they can call back in the morning."

"Hey ma, dad, are you up." Came blaring out from the answering machine in their bedroom. "Come on I know your home, I don't need to borrow money this time." He continued.

"On second thought, why not." Doyle said as he followed behind Mr. and Mrs. Smith into the bedroom, pushing them along so they didn't miss the call. "As a matter of fact I'll take the call for you." Doyle grabbed the phone, "Hey son!"

"Who is this?"

"Is this George Smith?"

"What do you want, where is my mother and father?"

"Your mother and father is right here where they need you to be. Now where are you?"

"I'm not telling you, what do you want me for?"

"We just need to ask you a couple of questions."

"About what?"

"Just tell me where you're at and we will bring you to your parents."

"Don't talk to me like no damn child." He said angrily, "And I know what this is about, that building that blew up isn't it?"

"Mr. Smith take it easy, we know you didn't have anything to do with that. Maybe you saw something that could help us." Doyle said and they went back and forth until Doyle's face turned red, frustrated by all the questions. He rested the phone on his shoulder and pulled a silencer out of his pocket. He seemed unruffled as he placed the silencer on the gun like the prospect of violence calmed him.

"Your mother dies in ten minutes and your father in fifteen and you will be dead within the next twenty four hours, I guarantee."

"Alright, alright I'm right here." Everyone turned to the sound of the voice that came from behind them. Both Doyle and O' Patrick had a look of bewilderment but Doyle tried to keep his wit about him. "Special Agent Black I didn't know you were kin to the Smiths," Doyle said as he repositioned himself behind Mr. Smith. SAB pocketed his cell phone and raised his gun to shoulder level pointing at Doyle. "You're not in Iraq, you forgot how it works around here?" SAB asked as he tried to maneuver around Mr. Smith for a clear shot. After they did a brief foot shuffle that ended up with Mr. Smith stuck in the middle SAB still didn't have a shot. SAB noticed the blood running down Mr. Smith's arm and he was looking faint.

The entire ride from the restaurant to the Smith's house SAB tried to think up another approach where he didn't have to cross the line and go against the grain, but he couldn't let them go around killing people like they were in Iraq or in some third world country. There was nothing favorable he could factor into this especially after the journalist told SAB how Cortex was using him to do their killing.

SAB hoped Doyle would make his decision easier and he did in that moment of query. Doyle's weight shifted from his right to his left and he was holding his gun in his left hand aiming straight for SAB's heart. At that very moment Mr. Smith fainted, dropping to the floor like a handkerchief in a drag race leaving nothing but air between Doyle and Special Agent Black.

Doyle got off two shots. SAB only had enough time to get off one before the slugs ripped into his chest sending him flying backwards. McCarthy, then Brinsky filtered into the room and Agent Walton followed. McCarthy ran down on O' Patrick while

Brinsky went after Doyle to find him leaning against a night table with a hole in his head. She quickly turned to SAB while Walton assisted with O' Patrick.

O' Patrick held his position safely behind Mrs. Smith. "So partner, how does this chapter end?" O' Patrick asked McCarthy referring back to a previous conversation they had on choosing between loyalty to ones profession or to one's life.

"I choose life, I'll be retiring soon. But it's your decision that concerns me." McCarthy replied in a low thoughtful tone as he looked into O' Patrick's eyes for a hint. O' Patrick winked at McCarthy, "My profession is my life." O' Patrick said as he flung Mrs. Smith into McCarthy and Walton's line of fire and turned his gun on Special Agent Black.

Before O' Patrick could get off a shot you heard two prickling sounds of glass from Mrs. Smith's window and O' Patrick dropped face down at SAB's feet.

## CHAPTER TEN

**Not even seconds after O' Patrick hit the floor** Special Agent Black's cell phone rang. It was an Agent Tinsely from Counter Terrorism Task Force, Northern District Office. "You found a body earlier today, he was ours."

"You mean Alfred Solomon, he came up a lot of things but nothing said he was Federal, what's going on?" SAB asked while pulling slugs out of the chest of his vest.

Tinsely explained that Solomon wasn't actually a federal agent per se, Solomon was an informant entrusted to handle special cases. In this case he was simply instructed to blend in and report what was said on the pulpit and find out why there were so many trips made from different members of the Mosque to Iraq, Saudi Arabia and Afghanistan.

At least that was the cover story. Now that Solomon was dead, that was the only story. This gave Agent Tinsely grounds to get the warrants he needed. Coupled with the fact Sandi's name was mentioned in some capacity. Finally Tinsely hit pay dirt and he was ready to apprehend some terrorist, the career break he has been waiting for.

Special Agent Blacks name was attached to the package which meant he had to be briefed on what he did now know about the members of the mosque they were preparing to invade. SAB also had to be debriefed. Tinsely needed a heads up on the mosque new member, Sandi.

While agents Brinsky and Simms brought in George Smith for questioning, McCarthy and SAB made it to the briefing.

Agent Tinsely went over a file he compiled over the past two years he has been watching this Mosque and its members. Over that two year period he used federal agents who would go in under cover. That was stopped by the Bureau because these tactics were ruled entrapment by the Supreme Court.

Then he resorted to relying on snitches who knew members of the Mosque. The Bureau averaged thirty two arrest per day in the Nouthern District. Twenty seven of those arrestees would disclose fractions of information that would prove helpful in locating and even arresting fugitives.

Once the arrestees proved reliable and willing to further their career as informants, they were then allowed to participate in the Bureau's Help Yourself Program. Arrestees would not have to serve their sentence for assistance in making more arrest that ended with a felony conviction.

Solomon was arrested on the front side of a fraud investigation. To avoid indictment and a mandatory 10 year sentence, he had to confess to his crime and include all involved.

His cooperation brought about 19 arrest, 13 of those plead guilty immediately thereafter and the remaining 6 eventually plead guilty. Solomon was then entitled to a reduced sentence of 5 years as a result of his 5K1 cooperation package. And since he proved to be reliable he was eligible for the second part of the program that only those who are not deemed a threat to society or a flight risk.

ANTHONY BREWER

Technically since Solomon single handedly brought down a whole fraud ring he was supposed to be set free, but Solomon took an interest in working for the Bureau. Solomon who was of Arab decent, was a Christian and more than willing to assist Agent Tinsely in "Apprehending those bad Muslims that give Arabs a bad rap." end of quote.

That's when Agent Tinsely gave Solomon an opportunity to further his career with the Bureau as an informant. He would be granted his release and receive a stipend based on the information he provided.

Solomon fit in immediately, he spoke Arabic and knew the basics of the religion of Islam. He was liked and even regarded as humble and pious because he spoke little of worldly things. He always sat in the Mosque around the brothers always listening, offering advice and praying with the congregation.

If Solomon was successful in providing the Bureau with information in this terrorist investigation, Solomon would have been provided with a bonus and visa granted to his ailing mother in Iraq. Solomon was on the job for 7 months prior to his untimely demise.

Agent Tinsely made up a list of suspects that were to be detained in connection to the murder of Alfred Solomon and suspected terrorist activity. *'Finally something that didn't have the smell of Cortex all over it,'* SAB thought as he and McCarthy sat and listened to the briefing.

All the men sought after besides Sandi were of African American decent. Two of which matched the description given by the two police officers and FBI agents that were attacked during the abduction of Sandi's niece and nephew. SAB called in one of the agents who would be able to make an identification and also lend a hand since the rest of his team were out chasing other leads.

Agent Tinsely dispatched three teams, he and SAB made the fourth. It was 1:21 AM when they surrounded the Mosque. The first floor could have been a store front like the surrounding buildings in the area, but since it was a Mosque the first floor was used for praying, sermons and open meetings. Previous Intel suggested that an office used by the Imam and a room where woman gathered was on the second floor. The Imam and his family lived on the third floor.

The first two teams moved quickly into the Mosque with no resistance. By the time Abdul the Mosque keeper was aware of the invasion the third team was already on their way in.

Abdul was quickly subdued as the teams split and spread throughout the Mosque, the fourth team went straight for the second floor while the first floor was secured.

"That's far enough." A man at the top of the stairs called out while firmly gripping a Ruger .357 Magnum.

"Drop your weapon, FBI." Agent Tinsely demanded as he flashed his identification in his one hand and pointed his glock with the other.

"Private property, you're invading my space." The man quickly retorted. SAB raised up the warrant he held in his hand. "If you're

Imam Ibraheem, this warrant is to search your Mosque. Now for the last time, put down the gun!"

In one motion Imam Ibraheem popped out the cylinder and dropped the shells from the .357 into his hand emptying the gun. "I have a license for this and the Mosque is downstairs," He advised.

"The warrant is for this entire premise," Agent Tinsely instructed as he began climb the steps.

"Please, my wife and young son is on the third floor." The Imam said as he gestured by handing the agent the gun.

Agent Tinsely didn't have a warrant for the Imam, only his son and nephew. Tinsely instructed the agents to continue their search while he and SAB searched the third floor. They then followed the Imam down to his office and questioned him on the whereabouts of his son and nephew and what he knew about Alfred Solomon.

The Imam's answer to the first question was simple. "You're asking me where is my son Idris and my nephew Hussein?" The Imam looked at his watch. "Almost two in the morning, I was hoping they were down stairs where I seen them last. As for your second question Alfred Solomon. Are you sure you don't mean Sulliman?" The Imam asked with a strained look.

Tinsely stepped forward and dropped a photo on the desk before the Imam. It was the pale looking Alfred Solomon. The second photo was of a lively Alfred Solomon who was in the company of members of the mosque, Idris being amongst them. Though there was nothing incriminating about that photos Agent Tinsely showed him, it was Agent Tinsely's implied threat that concerned the Imam more.

Threats that an innocent man with a wife and child had to consider. Especially at a time when you were guilty till proven guilty, especially when it came to being a Black Muslim in America.

This persecution of Muslims was once only relegated towards Arab Muslims, now any and every Muslim was a target like in the days of the crusades. He was not going to let his young son and wife be persecuted just because or for something his son did or did not do.

Aside from the usual claims of terrorism the fact remained a man was killed. By the Imams estimate that was a serious offence that warranted his cooperation. He picked up his phone, pressed a number he had in storage and tossed his phone to Agent Tinsely. "I don't know how much he can help you, or is willing to for that matter, but I done my part."

Tinsely snatched the phone out of the air and looked at the name and number on display it read "Ibn" that quickly translated in Tinsely's mind to mean son or Junior. He quickly placed the phone to his ear, the line was busy. Tinsely ended the call and pressed redial, it was still busy. Tinsely turned to SAB with a hopeful look on his face, "He must be on the line with someone."

Tinsely called the number into headquarters for a trace. As long as Idris stayed on the phone his signal could be picked up to an exact location. Within moments Tinsely had a general location where the signal was coming from.

SAB, McCarthy and Miller stayed behind to question the Imam. Tinsely and the rest of his men went after Idris. There was the chance if they found one of them, they found them all.

"How long has Sandi been a member of this Mosque?" SAB asked the Imam out of nowhere trying to catch him off guard. The Imam studied SAB trying to understand the question. He stood and came from behind his desk and approached SAB and McCarthy.

"My responsibility is to my family and the people of this community. Because of that responsibility I did not allow anything my son is accused of bring unnecessary hardship or trouble to them. For that same reason I would not allow someone known to blow up innocent people into this Mosque."

It was a reach, but he tried. It was obvious already that whatever Idris was into he kept from his father, which was usually the case in families where the father knew better and the son had to learn better on his own. SAB called Agent Tinsely to get his location and was told Idris's signal was coming from Long Island. Before jumping to any conclusions SAB asked the Imam did he know of any family or business that Idris had in Long Island.

From the lines forming across the Imams forehead it was apparent that he was giving SAB's question some serious thought. "No." He said shaking his head. "Not at this time of night," He added.

Aside from the war path that Agent Tinsely built up on his own, SAB was getting that gut feeling that Idris was in Long Island with Sandi and not the other way around.

## *TERRORIST IN BROOKLYN*

The culmination of events from the body found in a Brooklyn park with Sandi's name on it. Sandi's niece and nephew suddenly disappearing with the help of African Americans of course and now these same African Americans in Long Island where the Trocoby building is located.

SAB told McCarthy that he had a feeling they could be heading back to the Mosque. SAB called Brinsky, Simms, Jenkins and Walton to sit around with McCarthy and wait.

SAB felt something pulling him to Long Island. What he couldn't explain, it was how he knew Idris was in Long Island with the Sandi and that they were heading back to Brooklyn. It didn't make sense for SAB to go to the Trocoby Building if he thought they were coming back, but he had to go with his gut feeling.

## CHAPTER ELEVEN

**The phone rang out five, six times** on the seventh ring, "Yeah maintenance," A voice answered.

"I am going to provide you and the people around you with some very valuable information, but you cannot panic."

"Okay shoot," The maintenance man replied.

"In less than three minutes the building you are in will explode. You must calmly inform your coworkers and anyone else in the building."

"Who the hell is this?" the maintenance man screamed into the phone pissed someone was trying to pull a crank 2:01 in the morning. "Get the fuck out the building it's going to blow!" Hassan yelled back.

It had to be the dramatic way Hassan said it the second time that caused the maintenance man to drop the phone and run through the basement screaming "Bomb" "Bomb" as he made his way to the exit on the upper level.

If his coworkers napping in the next room did not hear him yelling they would have been left. The two night security guards watched him run pass their station like a flash of light. He ran smack into the glass side door exit the night crew used to get in and out of the building that was usually open.

He practically bounced off of the inch and a half thick glass door and turned to the security guards with tears in his eyes, "Open the god damn door it's a bomb, this place is going to blow!"

Both guards looked at each other knowing why all of a sudden this building needed extra security, they both hopped out their seats. One buzzed the door, the other grabbed his cell phone.

"I'll call this in when we hit the street," He said as they took off almost colliding into the last two maintenance men heading for the exit.

The maintenance men didn't make it far once outside the building before they were clobbered and knocked to the ground. The security guards quickly drew their weapons and upon realizing it was an ambush, they quickly dropped their guns at the sight of the larger automatic weapons.

The two security guards and maintenance men were taken back into the building then secured in the trash compact room in the basement. Al Amin who was already dressed in a security uniform manned the security station in the front lobby while Hassan, Hussein and Idris returned to the truck.

They returned through the basement with four large cases on pullies, three shoulder bags and Sandi. They unloaded ammonium nitrate from the four cases, emptied the contents of two of the shoulder bags and Hassan and Hussein got into the elevator leaving Sandi and Idris in the basement to prepare the explosives.

The way they had it planned, Idris and Sandi would set up the Bomb in the boiler room since according to their chemical engineer that would be the best supply of energy to fuse with the ammonium nitrate to topple the building. Then Sandi and Idris would go to the eighth floor to assist Hassan and Hussein remove, an unspecified amount of cash from the holding room, they were told was there.

"Was told" and "unspecified amount" was the terminology used, which meant nothing was verified, they didn't have time to. After Sandi poured out his heart about how his family was murdered over oil by this billion dollar conglomerate, which according to Sandi was responsible for the mass murder of Muslims in Iraq. This struck a nerve amongst these men who considered themselves Muhajideens, soldiers of God.

All of the men traveled back and forth to one country or another on a regular that occupied mostly Muslim populations. Each mans travels took him to different places for different reasons at different points in their lives in a quest to better learn and understand their religion.

The average Muslim made Hajj and had no other desires to take such a lengthy, not to mention costly trip to the Middle East. To be amongst an Arab people who believed they were better people and better Muslims then the African American Muslims.

Idris the son of an Imam, his cousin and a large percentage of the African American Muslim population didn't see it that way. Since Islam is to be learned at the feet of Islamic scholars, they have been going back and forth to various Islamic countries for years to learn from Islamic Sheiks so they can in turn teach their brothers and sisters in America properly.

During these years they not only learned the religion, they bonded with their brothers and sisters of the same faith as the

Quran prescribed to *"Hold on to the rope of Allah, that is far reaching and a bond of strength."*

Over the year each of them held that rope a little tighter than others, but all the same explained the pain they felt at the all too familiar reports of how so many Muslims were being murdered throughout the Middle East. Sandi struck gold in this sympathetic bunch.

Idris was the first to sign on, his cousin on the other hand was reluctant. It wasn't because he was older then Idris that made him somewhat more rational. It had more to do with the history of Muslims killing of Muslims and America killing Muslims before his little crew was born.

What difference would it make them jumping out there when chances are whatever they did would not make a difference now or later. Since Al Amin and a few other brothers were hinging on Hussein's vote Idris asked his cousin to at least consider it, for him.

While Hussein thought about it, Idris went ahead and did what he could do without Hussein, he snatched Sandi's niece and nephew. After Idris made that move he practically committing them. Hussein went to the Trocoby building to see what they were up against.

Going into the Trocoby building he bumped into an old associate he once went to school with. He was coming from the personnel department filling out a few applications when he seen Hussein. "Commodities and acquisitions is what I hope for, but from what I hear of this place I'll get stuck in paper work."

"What do you mean the mail room?" Hussein asked.

"Na, shredding or invoices. But if I had my wish, I would pick the holding room."

*"The holding room?"* that was the first time Hussein heard of it and though he knew he didn't have the most reliable source, these millions in profits for the outrageous gas prices had to go somewhere. Everybody knew all the money never went straight to the bank.

Since Idris was going to persuade him to go anyway, at least Hussein had his own reasons that benefited a lot more people than Sandi and his cause at the end of the day.

Stealing was what Idris called it when informed by Hussein about the holding room and a lecture followed on how many men with good intentions are marred by such acts. Hussein usually held his tongue because he didn't mind hearing the religious angle Idris would always throw out there to put things into perspective, but not this time.

"Have you been watching the same war for oil I have been watching?" Hussein asked Idris angrily amazed he would even go there when it was Idris begging him to come.

"This is not a game you signed us up for. We keep the spoils or you call this off." Was Hussein's last words and there was no need for him to explain to Idris how bad they would need that money if this deed came back on them and they needed to leave town.

Al Amin was able to watch Idris and Sandi in the Basement preparing the explosives and at the same time watch Hassan and Hussein as they stepped off the elevator on the 8th floor.

They went straight to work blowing off the first door to the holding room. As soon as they touched the second door leading to the holding room the red lights on Al Amin's security monitor began flickering for the $8^{th}$ floor silent alarm.

Al Amin sat and curiously watched the blinking red light wondering if anyone else could see it. In one minute and seven seconds later that question was answered by the ringing phone at his station. It was the buildings Systems Operating Security Management that seen the alarm and called in for a confirmation.

This at least gave him something to work with and he didn't have to worry about a bunch of police running through the front door. Since there was suppose to be two guards on duty his first response was that he sent his partner to take a look see. "I'll give you a call back once we confirm something either way," Al Amin told the man on the other end of the phone.

"No I'll wait. Do you have a visual of your partner?"

"Yes he is approaching now," Al Amin replied then paused as if he was really waiting for a confirmation.

While Al Amin was stalling, the Security Operating Systems Manager was already sending support staff since Al Amin didn't follow protocol. Al Amin didn't know he couldn't confirm without requesting an access code from the S.O.M.S. when they called.

What was worse the S.O.M.S didn't suppose call the Trocoby building, whoever was working was suppose to know protocol and call and inform S.O.M.S and inform them of the possible breach or in the least give notification of a false alarm.

After a minute passed Al Amin advised that everything was fine and that it had to be an electrical glitch. S.O.M.S agreed and told Al Amin to reset the alarm and hung up. And in good time, a blast from the eighth floor echoed through the building.

"What the hell was that?" Idris asked hearing the explosion all the way in the basement.

"We just blew the vault," Hassan replied fighting off a cloud of debris and dust.

Seemed everyone else's job was going according to plan and Al Amin was the only one with problems. "Plan B" he calmly whispered into his headset. "Confirm, plan B." Al Amin repeated unsure if his first command was heard.

As soon as he heard both confirmations from the basement and the eighth floor he disengaged the buildings alarm system so they could make their exits from different parts of the building undetected if needed.

Then he tended to his next chore, he had to give a welcome to the two cars that pulled up in front of the building. One of the cars pulled in front of the only car parked in front of the Trocoby building and the other pulled behind it. They parked bumper to bumper in an attempt to lock it in, as if they knew it belonged to the could be intruders. What they didn't know was that car was filled with explosives in the event something like this happened and they needed to clear the way.

They were there longer then they needed to be so it was time to go anyway. 'Maybe a little fireworks would move things along,' Al Amin thought as picked up the remote control detonator and watched two men get out of each car like they were doing a drill, done over and over again armed with what looked like 9 MM H&K Uzi's.

Al Amin pointed the remote at the door as he watched the surveillance monitor, before he could set off the fireworks he noticed Taliban from the corner of the screen walking slowly towards the suits. The four suits that were focused on their task at hand did not see him coming from their far left.

Taliban raised his hand from his side, in it he held a Smith & Wesson .357, the sound of it echoed through the empty street. The power of it ripped through the rib cage of the closest man to him knocking him into the two others.

Taliban raised his other hand that carried the identical .357 that sounded louder to the other three men as they began to scurry for cover. Only two of them were partially successful almost making it back to their cars as Taliban cut them down with back shots.

Taliban was breathing through his nose, his chest rose high with every breath as he approached the two men that laid face down. "Look at me," He yelled kicking the first one he came to and shot him in the face as he tried to look over his shoulder at his assailant.

The second man wasted no time looking behind him as he attempted to crawl away. Taliban stepped on his back and pulled the trigger. Taliban turned and looked towards the entrance of the building. He could not see Al Amin but he was sure Al Amin saw him.

"What's our status?" came over the headset.

"We're walking out the front door but we have to go now." Al Amin instructed.

"On our way." Idris replied, than Hussein confirmed that he heard the instructions and was on his way.

Al Amin watched as Taliban picked up the automatic weapons of the men he killed. "Bring the truck around," Al Amin demanded. Without a reply Taliban returned to the truck carrying the weapons on his shoulder as boldly as if he was in Afghanistan.

Al Amin gave him that name Taliban. Unlike the rest of the crew Al Amin never traveled back and forth to Muslim countries. He made Hajj once and was satisfied with the experience and fulfilled his religious obligation. He didn't want to be like an Arab or act like one, the Arabs had their culture and the black man had their own. He knew where to draw the line between culture and religion at least for him, Taliban was a whole other story.

Hussein, Hassan, Idris and Sandi all exited the elevator with pullies and shoulder bags bigger than the ones they came in with. "How are you going to make it out of here with all that?" Al Amin asked.

"Who is going to stop me?" Hussein asked sarcastically. Al Amin turner and pointed to the two blue and white police cars coming to a screeching halt with sirens blazing.

Hussein dropped everything he was carrying except the AK 47 strapped across his back and he ran out of the building. With one foot in the car and one foot out, the cop on the driver side didn't know where to go for cover.

Hussein helped him along as he squeezed the trigger of the AK 47 and shells started flying. The cop jumped into the car and crawled out the passenger side where his partner was trying to return fire that was nothing compared to what the AK 47 was spitting out.

Both cops jumped into the second police car that came on the scene to assist them and "BANG" Taliban collided head on with them smashing them into another car. The collision caused an explosion on impact. Taliban climbed onto the sidewalk with his monster truck and went to pick up his companions.

They started loading the truck but the police would not stop coming. NYPD, Nassau County police and a number of unmarked cars that had to be FBI filled with suits. Taliban wasted no time, he draped an AK 47 over his shoulder then grabbed two of the H&K Uzis he picked up earlier from the dead suits and grinned as if he knew they would make all his problems go away.

Al Amin stopped Taliban and Hussein who seemed to be racing to engage the police in battle. Al Amin wanted to scorn them for wanting to run out there like suicide bombers with no regard for life, like they didn't have alternatives.

Agent Tinsely arrived on the scene and immediately called for medical assistance and back up as he, his agents and supporting police tried to position themselves around the dead bodies and cars of the first and second response teams who arrived only moments earlier.

## CHAPTER TWELVE

**F.B.I. Deputy Director Walter Ramen** stepped out of his home with his morning cup of java to retrieve his daily paper and found two men outside his door, one of which was standing on his paper. "Mr. Dercole wants to see you," One of the men instructed.

The Deputy Director turned to go back into his house, "Now!" the other man who stood 6' 3" square chinned, wearing a dark gray suit demanded as he placed his hand on the Deputy Director's shoulder stopping him from going back into his safe haven. Ramen gave a smirk, pulled his door shut, turned and casually walked over to a limousine that awaited them.

One man got into the front, the other into the back with Mr. Ramen and there Mr. Dercole sat patiently waiting. Mr. Dercole handed the Deputy Director a folder that was handed to him only moments after returning from Texas with a meeting with Mr. Richard. The folder provided surveillance reports and the estimated damages to Cortex in the last twenty four hours. Damages included a body count that exceeded thirteen men.

"Are you accepting the responsibility for that?" Dercole asked as he watched Ramen flip through the pages. Ramen looked up from the folder with a bewildered look on his face. "Doyle and O' Patrick are dead?" The Deputy Director asked as if not believing what he was reading.

"I can't quite remember the conversation, but I was leaning towards wiping out the rest of the Blacks and I recall you thought a promotion would make the problem go away. Now do you suppose you give him your job or the Directors?" Dercole added to wipe that dumb lost look off of the Deputy's face like he didn't understand the score.

"And it did go away!" Ramen retorted in his defense. "It was your arrogance that made him a problem. This is not Iraq and Black is still a federal agent. How much did you expect him not to see?" Ramen added.

Dercole didn't come for a debate. The orders came straight down from Mr. Richard himself, it was time to wrap this up.

The new administration was coming in and the loose ends had to be cleaned up. This new President was sure to be around for two terms and Richards wanted to be on the same team despite his ties with the past Borish administration.

"You tried it your way, now we do it mines. Take his badge and we'll take care of the rest."

\*       \*       \*       \*       \*       \*       \*       \*       \*

**10:30 Monday morning,** four U.S. Marshals walked into Special Agent Blacks office and disrupted there meeting. "Special Agent Christopher Black?" the first Marshal that came through the door asked as he surfed faces from agent to agent.

All five agents turned and looked at the Marshals as if to say whose asking. The Marshals flashed their tin stars. McCarthy was the first to address them, telling them what they already figured by canvassing the office since no one of African American decent was present.

"Do you know where we could locate Agent Black?" the Marshal asked.

"That's exactly what we are trying to figure out now." Agent Walton replied as he got up to introduce himself. The Marshals that was standing in the rear stepped up and brushed pass Agent Walton like he was a piece of office furniture as they made their way to Agent Brinsky, practically pushing Agent Simms aside who was standing next to her.

"Agent Brinsky I am U.S. Marshal Lawrence. Do you have any idea where we can find Agent Black?" The Marshal paused waiting for an answer, than cut her off before she could utter a word. He warned her and the other agents that aiding and abetting a known terrorist, is an act of terrorism itself and would be prosecuted as treason.

McCarthy, Simms, Walton, Jenkins and Brinsky all looked at him like he spoke an alien language. Now that he gave his warning he thought it appropriate to repeat his question.

"And this time before you think to answer Agent Brinsky, I would also advise we are aware of the personal relationship between you and Agent Black," The Marshal added as he handed Agent Brinsky photos of her and Agent Black entering his co-op.

"What the hell is going on here?" McCarthy demanded as he faced off with Marshal Lawrence. The allegations, the threats and now pressing the rookie, McCarthy heard enough.

"Calm down Agent McCarthy, I can understand your frustration but-"

"Frustration, you come up in here with your noses in the air slinging bullshit like we're civilians. We hunt the same marks and collect a check from the same Uncle Sam. Now what the fuck is going on?" McCarthy demanded staring down the Marshals.

The four Marshals looked at McCarthy, all but one was younger, ranging from 27 to 42 years old. McCarthy superseded all of them in rank, experience and field work.

The Marshals knew that before they walked into the office looking for SAB. They had to know who would be loyal and who would be their biggest opposition.

The senior Marshal finally spoke up as if he came along for the sole purpose of handling McCarthy, or because of his grayish white hair whatever he said would be more believable. "Khalif Ibn Sajud born 1973 at Kings County hospital to Mariam Sajud and Raheem Sajud. You know Khalif Sajud by his most common name Christopher Black, Special Agent Black or SAB." The Marshal stepped forward and handed Agent McCarthy a warrant he pulled out of his inside coat pocket.

It was a federal warrant signed by a federal judge for the arrest of Christopher Black for acts of Treason against the Unite States of America and conspiring to commit terrorist activity. McCarthy glanced at the warrant like a flier someone tries to shove in your hand while walking in a shopping mall. The Marshals saw the look on McCarthy's face then passed the warrant to Simms who was standing next to him.

"The Bureau has been watching his activity for a year now. Because he is one of ours we were cautious, but now we have enough to bring him in." The Marshal said gesturing by nodding his head to say, Feds to Feds that's the courtesy you requested. "Now it's your turn, where is he?" he asked.

"That's the first question you asked and never waited for an answer. If you would have I would have told you we too are looking for him and haven't seen him since last night's catastrophe." Agent Brinsky replied handing the Marshal the photos he shoved in her face.

"In any event-" McCarthy chimed in. "I'm sure some of the information we have acquired working with Special Agent Black could be useful to the investigation or in locating him. Like I said we are all on the same team."

FBI protocol under the circumstances required the agents who worked with Agent Black to be debriefed at the soonest possible time, usually before the continuation of duties depending on the nature of the charges of the agent being investigated.

This debriefing could be put off under the guise of seeking counsel or departmental advice. In this case it was the opposite, they wanted to know what the story was so the debriefing was their only way of being briefed first hand on SAB's alleged activities.

The only problem being no one called for a debriefing. McCarthy found this very unusual, considering the nature of the charges against a lead agent responsible for one of the biggest cases since the world trade center bombing.

No one called, not even the Office of Professional Responsibility or Internal Affairs. It was business as usual. McCarthy who was leading the pack in SAB's absence decided to focus on finding SAB. "If there is anything else brewing i'm sure we'll hear about it." He said discounting the Marshals visit.

Whether or not they believed any of the allegations was another story. Despite the trust they had in their team leader, they still had to contend with one thing that was proven about Special Agent Black, his name was Khalif Ibn Sajud and he was a Muslim. Minutes before seeing that file they would have sworn that to be impossible.

"Could that be why he was so..." Agent Walton stopped and his forehead wrinkled as he strained searching for a word to describe SAB's antisocial behavior.

"Aloof?" Simms replied than looked at Agent Walton with a game show face to see if he chose the right word. Everyone was on pins and needles not wanting to say anything anti-SAB because it was obvious they all were far from a verdict in the case of United States of America v. Christopher Black a.k.a. Khalif Ibn Sajud.

"Brinsky what do you think?" Jenkins asked. All focus was now on her after Marshals accusations that she and SAB were shacking up.

"Think about what?" She asked lost in her own thoughts.

"Hello are you with us, Simms said aloof. Since you spent the most time with him lately, what do you think?"

"No, that's not true. But I was just thinking about the time we spent together." She replied as she stood up like she had somewhere to go. "If you fellahs hear something give me a call, I have to see a man about a horse!"

They all looked at Agent Brinsky as she left the office then looked at each other. They all knew that was an expression SAB used regularly.

Agent Brinsky jumped in her car and headed to Long Island. The last time anyone heard from SAB he was on his way to the Trocoby Center. By the time they all reached the Trocoby Center it was already demolished from the explosion.

Something kept telling her to go back to Long Island. She didn't know that was the same voice in her head that caused SAB to disappear.

She knew SAB always had a hard time finding the Trocoby Center. There was a short cut she showed him and she was sure he took it, that was the way she went hoping she would see something.

She turned on the radio to get a glimpse of current events and see if there was anything was being said about the charges against SAB. The radio helped her relax as she cruised on the Expressway and thought about what has transpired over the last couple of weeks since the names Sandi and Cortex surfaced.

She turned up the radio when she heard something about a journalist in Iraq. She thought about the meeting her and SAB had with the Journalist Pandora.

Pandora told them stories of how journalist were killed in Iraq to silence reports of atrocities committed against innocent Iraqis who played no part in the war games, but were dying. The last report of civilian casualties in the last eight years in Iraq alone was 2.7 million.

"In other journalist related news, Noble Laureate Lillian Dalton has died. She is known for her uncompromising reporting of the crimes against the Bosnian people and the Iran - Iraq Crisis. She will be remembered."

Agent Brinsky couldn't take her eyes off the radio, she couldn't believe what she just heard. By the time she looked up she was a few feet away from colliding into the back of a pick-up truck. She swerved out of the lane and stepped on the gas as she darted through the traffic and off the Expressway.

As she got close to her destination she slowed down and her eyes combed the streets. At the same time she tried to clear her mind and conjure a thought of her own because all that came to mind was everyone else's thoughts and opinions and why they thought it.

She had to pull over. She couldn't drive, scan the streets, think about what the Marshals said, what Pandora said and think how all this played into what has translated into SAB being charged as a terrorist.

From where she was she could see the Trocoby Center, at least where it was or what was left of it. She was close enough, so she parked and walked in a slow moderate pace as she again tried to sort her thoughts. There were fire trucks, emergency units, ambulances and special units to remove the debris.

The emergency units stayed on standby with hopes some of the bodies removed from the rubbish would be alive. They had no way of knowing all the people died before the building came down. The area was barricaded so Brinsky stood on the perimeter with the other bystanders and watched as the special units meticulously worked to remove the debris and placed it into trucks and other secured areas.

The bystanders watched with wide eye focus on the area where the big machines were pulling cars from under the fallen debris. Some cars were buried deeper than others depending how close they were at the time the building collapsed. In other areas the ground opened up and the cars fell into the voids and debris fell on top of the cars. The crowd watched in awe as the large crane pulled the cars out of the cavities.

Agent Brinsky recognized one of the cars as a federal issued vehicle. One side of it was torched and the roof crushed. She flashed her credentials as she took a step forward to bypass the barriers for a closer look. Brinsky immediately looked away from the car that was being lowered. The sight of the man hanging from the burnt vehicle was too much for her. He was burnt to a charcoal black with glass protruding through his upper body and face.

Brinsky regained her composure and headed to the outpost set up as a command station. *But what am I looking for?* she asked herself as she watched the State and Federal agencies shuffling back and forth looking for answers of their own. She stopped in her tracks and back peddled the moment she realized whatever answer she was looking for was not going to come from them.

She was distracted by a bunch of bystanders who watched from the perimeter. They were shouting something and pointing to another car the crane pulled out of a cavity. Brinsky couldn't understand what the people were shouting, but then it became obvious when she looked up at the car dangling fifteen feet in the air swaying back and forth.

"He's going to make the car fall." Someone yelled out.

The crane operator stopped everything the moment he heard that, but they were not talking about him. The windshield of the car came flying down crashing onto a pile of rubble and a man dropped from the car. He landed on his feet crouched down with bended knees in a cat position to brake his fall.

He stood up straight and looked around for a moment as if he were lost. He was looking for identifying marks something to tell him where he was. The sight reminded him of Oklahoma and how that building was blown up and collapsed to nothing but rubbish.

The bystanders quietly stood and watched to see what the man would do next. An African American man from amongst the crowd slowly worked his way to the front. He silently tried to get the man's attention by removing his hat and waving it at him but it didn't work.

"Sajud" The man called out. The man who stood on the pile of debris looked and without hesitation leaped down from the pile of rocks and dirt and ran towards the crowd.

Agent Brinsky tried not to lose the man as he made it through the crowd. It wasn't until the two men headed to a car that Brinsky realized she didn't have her car and panic set in, but not for long. A man pulled up in a Federal Emergency Management Agency truck and left it running to retrieve something from the back of his truck and it pulled off without him.

Brinsky tried to stay a safe distance behind them as she trailed on the expressway in her big blue sport utility van with the red F.E.M.A decal.

"How did you know I would be here?"

"You're a federal agent assigned to terrorist activity. I think a building getting blown up qualifies."

"No, I think you lucked up."

"No I didn't," the man replied as he reached into his glove compartment and pulled out an envelope. "How long have you been buried alive?"

SAB looked at the clock on the dash board. "About seven hours."

"Well I don't know where I should start."

"You start can by telling me what made you come looking for me after what, eight months or so."

The man swerved over and took the next exit off the expressway and pulled over the first chance he got. "First of all boy, I don't have to explain nothing to you. It's my name on your birth certificate and you're damn sure past the age of me looking for you. Remember you're the big bad FBI man." Mr. Black Sr. tossed the envelope into Special Agent Blacks lap.

"Which reminds me why I called you Sajud back there, the same reason you answered to it it's your name and your FBI buddies know it. And what I gather from them knocking on my door six o' clock this morning, they don't want to be friends with you anymore son."

After hearing that Sajud flung the envelope onto the dash board without opening it, pulled out his gun and jumped out the car. SAB noticed the suspicious blue truck swerve off the expressway when his father did.

SAB raised his gun when he seen the driver side door of the blue truck swing open. Agent Brinsky stepped out with her weapon raised and they stood in the middle of the street bearing down on each other.

"Holster your weapon!" SAB demanded.

"Khalif Ibn Sajud you drew your weapon first. Holster your weapon," She retorted without batting an eye.

SAB felt a sharp pain as if she let off a shot, that's how much hearing her calling him Sajud hurt him and she seen it in his eyes.

SAB knew he couldn't stand in the middle of the street with a gun in his hand much longer before drawing attention to himself. SAB holstered his weapon and left Brinsky standing in the street with her gun pointing at him.

Agent Brinsky put her gun away and walked around to the front of the car SAB got into. She instantly recognized Mr. Black Sr. from the crowd when he called out to Sajud, now she was standing face to face with him. Agent Brinsky stood there not knowing what to do. Mr. Black did not know her or why she was there. He put the car in drive and went to drive around her.

"Stop" she shouted as she jumped in front of the car extending her hand as if she could stop it manually. SAB quickly grabbed his father's shoulder and they came to an abrupt stop. Agent Brinsky slowly walked around to the passenger side of the car and stared at SAB for a moment, then got in without saying a word, her mind was made.

## CHAPTER THIRTEEN

**It was not how the Feds came into the Mosque** that made the Imam uneasy, it was the alarming manner in which they left.

Three Federal Agents and four NYPD hung around for support lingering aimlessly since the search was complete, they found nothing. Out of the blue they all broke into a frenzy. The Imam was sure it had everything to do with a radio transmission that sent them running like someone's life depended on them getting somewhere.

Whatever was going on he knew he could move undetected for the moment. He grabbed his son and his wife and moved quickly as if their lives counted on it and took them to a place of safety where no one would be able to find them. Then he went and looked for Idris the only one place he knew he could find him.

\*　　\*　　\*　　\*　　\*　　\*　　\*　　\*　　\*

Idris, Hussein, Hassan, Al Amin, Sandi and Kawi made it to Brooklyn. They already knew the Feds came to the Mosque looking for them. They already planned to go somewhere that no one would know to look for them, then after that they would move again but regardless where they went it would always be in Brooklyn where they could see anyone coming at them.

No one knew Hussein had a house because he lived with his cousin for as long as anyone could remember. The house was left

ANTHONY BREWER

to Hussein by his deceased parents and he never lived there. From time to time he would collect rent from it and that was it.

When they got to his house the first thing they did was turn on the news to see how much the police knew, while they busied themselves with counting the money they took from the Trocoby Center.

Kawi glanced over briefly and everyone was hypnotized by the television. With the exception of Hussein who was stacking the money into rows. Unconcerned with them Kawi began to neatly arrange all the artillery according to caliber and model.

The three MP5 Heckler & Koch he took off the dead bodies he favored because of the small size and power of these fully automatic weapons. He threw one MP5 in a duffel bag and another he placed around his neck and let it hang like by the strap like a rapper who wore an oversized chain and ridiculously large medallion. Then he put a sweat shirt over it to conceal it.

Al Amin watched as Kawi approached the large pile of money that stood at least three feet high seven feet wide. Kawi's eyes widened as he scanned the pile and reached in filling his duffel bag then headed towards the door.

"Why is he leaving?" Sandi asked when he seen the rest were ignoring Kawi.

"Since you're concerned maybe you should ask him," Al Amin replied.

"Taliban where you going?" Sandi asked. Kawi turned and gave Sandi a look but the phone rang and stopped Kawi from speaking.

No one knew they were there, which meant someone was coming. Hussein quickly grabbed the phone and listened. It was the brother they had posted on the street for look out telling Hussein Idris's father was coming.

"Imam Ibraheem is here." Hussein announced then hung the phone up with a sigh.

The Imam entered Hussein's house and paused in the doorway after closing it behind him. The shades were drawn keeping out all but a ray of light that divided the living room in half.

The Imam looked around at the faces that were watching him. Then he studied the arsenal of guns neatly arranged on the table off to the side. His eye's bounced from the guns to the money on the floor then to the only Arab in the room, Sandi.

The Imam would never assign guilt to anyone without first hearing that person's side of the story. Particularly in light of the fact that he too have been a victim of stereotypes, but a building was blown up and he was the only Arab there.

Everyone from Idris to Hassan was trained in one thing or another from hand to hand combat to weapons, but none of them were trained in explosives that could crumble a sixteen story building to dust.

Idris watched as his mild mannered and always humble father's body language started to change. It was obvious what he seen in his sister's house bothered him. Idris rose and greeted his father then said something in Arabic that translated into Idris asking his father into the next room to speak privately.

Sandi looked on surprised after hearing how fluent Idris spoke his native language. Kawi watched with interest as Imam Ibraheem followed Idris into the next room.

When the door closed behind them, Kawi opened the door in front of him. The Imams presence couldn't alter what already transpired, so he couldn't alter what came next, Kawi still had to prepare.

The conversation between Idris and his father was a dialogue between two generations of Muslims. Imam Ibraheem was the first in his family to accept Islam in the sixties. He was not a Nation of Islam convert like most older brothers from that time. Imam Ibraheem was from the first clan who got it straight from the Sheik on State Street in Brooklyn.

Knowing the value of the proper teachings of Islam the Imam sent his son abroad to learn the religion. Idris became just as knowledgeable as his father but the main difference between Idris and his father was the generation gap.

Which translated to a difference in how things were done, similar to the differences between how Reverend Dr. Martin Luther King Jr. and Malcolm X differed in their approach to doing things?

The Imam knew he didn't have the time to again argue these points with his son, the damage was already done. Instead he valued the time between them, he did not know the next time he would see his son.

## CHAPTER FOURTEEN

**Agent Brinsky had questions and she needed answers.** She decided she would do better listening and paying attention to where they were taking her. They had been on the highway for at least an hour before Mr. Black Sr. pulled off the highway and found his way to the old dirt road they traveled on.

"You read this?" SAB asked his father without lifting his eyes from the page.

Mr. Black shook his head. He couldn't get pass the disc that came with the papers. Pandora told SAB she was giving him information, what information was never made clear to him.

The envelope she gave him at the restaurant he never got a chance to read and now this, which didn't explain much aside from the obvious he learned thus far on his own, Cortex has government officials in their pockets.

None of this was enough to make Cortex go around killing people. Okay maybe some of the Senators listed with their party favors that put these corporations in positions for trillion dollar oil contracts.

Upon retirement these same government officials and Senators would sit pretty in the private sector they laid the laws and turned a blind eye for.

Mr. Black Sr. stopped in front of a cabin and popped the trunk. "The suit case in the trunk should help and this place here is off the map," Mr. Black Sr. said softly as he handed his son the keys.

Mr. Black Sr. looked up at his son with heavy eyes and mustard a smile. "When I listened to the disc last night I was going to find these mutual friends of ours and our lady Lillian Dalton.

But after hearing the news about you, I figured if they wanted my son, I'll give them my son. Now you give them hell. **You send them to hell!**" He bellowed. "You send them to hell." He repeated in a low voice then banged on the steering wheel in an attempt to hold back the tears from falling from his eyes.

Seeing his father distraught SAB knew he would find all the answers he sought in the disc. SAB hasn't seen his father like that since his mother died last year. *'Did this have something to do with his mother? That would be the only thing that could get him this worked up like this.'*

Mr. Black Sr. knew nothing about or would careless about Cortex and their business, what else could it be. SAB turned and looked at Agent Brinsky in the back seat who looked on overwhelmed by Mr. Black's distress. *'What did they do? What did they do?'* she wanted to ask Mr. Black Sr., feeling his pain but not knowing its cause.

She felt SAB's eyes on her and when she looked at him she seen he was about to tell her to go back with his father, she gave Mr. Black Sr. one final glance then rushed out of the car before SAB could say anything to her.

The rookie thought SAB was worried about her career. At the rate people were dying her career was the last thing on his mind, which made him shift back to his father who he knew was going back to Brooklyn.

SAB was an invert because his father was a bigger invert and whatever had his father near tears he knew his father would welcome whole heartily. SAB stood there for a moment as he watched his father drive off then went into the cabin.

He wasted no time once inside. He dropped the suit case and went to the seat closest to him which was at a table. He placed the disc player on the table and pressed play. Immediately he recognized the voice, he looked across the table at the empty chair as if she was sitting there talking to him in person. For that moment nothing else existed, not even Agent Brinsky who peered over his shoulder and listened like an uninvited intruder.

Lillian Dalton spoke loudly and she came across very clear, almost with the intent to antagonize SAB as she tried at the restaurant. "Special Agent Black, Mr. Christopher Black or would it be more fitting to call you as your mother named you Khalif Ibn Sajud.

For the purpose of this notification I would rather your short name SAB. Please be advised that henceforth you are under my employ and as previously instructed you will do my bidding."

SAB sat there almost comatose as he listened to her tell a story he thought he knew. SAB and his father were told that his mother Mariam S. Black died from an explosion in Iraq while attending a wedding. Accordingly, the bombing was a result of a rivalry between Sunni and Shi'a factions.

Agent Black a few years in the Bureau at the time, with his best effort could not retrieve his mother's body nor would his office allow him to go to Iraq and find answers. They said they needed him, so much so he was promoted which left a bad taste in his father's mouth ever since because even with the promotion the Bureau nor his FBI son couldn't tell him how or why his wife died.

According to Lillian Dalton, on August 10, 2010 the day of the wedding of the Salaams, Talib Abdul Rahman the chairman of Barakata Oils was finishing a meeting with an American oil company and was in route to the wedding when he and his translator was ambushed and killed.

By who was never known, but Talib Abdul Rahman's death allowed Barakata Oils to be acquired by an American oil company only days before the United Nations implemented a new oil policy prohibiting American oil companies from dictating contracts favorable to U.S. contractors who were making more money than the Iraqis that owned the oil.

That was then, now Cortex is right out blatantly taking over Desert land mining it for oil, then building complexes on top of it. **"They're not occupying anymore they're owning it,"** she said. American Industrial Oil Complex stationed in Iraq on top of Iraqi oil. Or is it Cortex's oil since it's on Cortex property, almost like squatting since anywhere on the planet knew position was nine tenths of the law.

With 200,000 U.S. Troops in Iraq and over 100,000 private military contractors with over 70 billion dollars spread out across Iraq buying politicians, warlords and Sheiks, who was going to stop them?

"Talib Abdul Rahman and his translator Mariam Sajud Black's bodies were never found. Less than an hour after they're murdered, the location where his family awaited him to attend the wedding was bombed. Conveniently the U.S. media reported that the Iraqi oil tycoon was killed at his wedding with the American, your mother."

"Why do I tell you this? Because it's in my best interest to enrage you with a thirst for revenge with the fact that your mother was not only murdered in cold blood, but they hid this from you, then insulted your intelligence by promoting you to divert your attention from your mother's senseless death. And to add further injury they have you work for the same people responsible for her murder."

"Are you upset yet Special Agent Black? I hope so because now I will tell you my bidding. The reason you are listening to this recording is because like your mother, I too was murdered in cold blood because of what I knew like Arif Salaam.

You got it, the poor guy Salaam who wanted to write a story that would expose the U.S. as terrorist finds his who family was killed.

Arif didn't have all the pieces, but he was the last of piece of the Salaam family puzzle. Cortex made sure of that or should I say you did?"

"All the information you need on Mr. Richards you will find enclosed, find him and kill him. Though it is my bidding you will still do it for your mother which is all the same *CHECK MATE* at the end of the game."

There was a short pause then she continued and gave SAB the last piece of the puzzle. She told him that the American oil company in Iraq then was called Lerrian Oils. After acquisition and consolidation of Barakata Oils they changed their name to Cortex International owned by Mr. Carlton Richard.

"It's all documented in Arif Salaams report that I finished for him due to his untimely demise. You have the proof, you know the score and it's time to get even. I painted a good picture for revenge, you can paint a better one for justice."

The recording stopped snapping SAB out of his comatose state as the figure across from him disappeared. SAB sat motionless trying to digest all that was unleashed upon him so sudden.

The entire time Agent Brinsky stood motionless behind SAB as she listened to the recording. Every time she heard a reference to SAB's murdered mother, the photo of Mrs. Black that sat on the mantel in SAB's living room came to mind. The intentionally cruel manner in which Pandora described the atrocity had Agent Brinsky on the verge of tears. She rolled her shoulders back and took a deep breath as she lifted her head high trying to fight back tears.

In the few minutes Agent Brinsky stood there, so many questions were answered and everything that happened in the last two weeks started to make sense. Particularly, in that few seconds O' Patrick had to take a shot at anyone in the room. When it was McCarthy and Brinsky bearing down on him, if he wanted to get away, why shoot Special Agent Black who was laid out and harmless at the moment.

Brinsky also understood why Lillian Dalton called herself Pandora. The Pandora box was now open and if Lillian Dalton had it her way Mr. Richard would be buried right next to her or because of her. It didn't matter as long as he was in a box six feet under.

Pandora laid it on SAB thick enough for him to want to go after Mr. Richard and Cortex. If Pandora would have mentioned how his mother was murdered in cold blood just once more, the near tears Agent Brinsky would have killed Mr. Richard herself.

But the fact remained SAB was useless to Pandora and himself. He was a most wanted by the FBI and Cortex which meant only one of two things, he would end up dead or in jail.

Agent Brinsky's cell phone rang, it was McCarthy. Brinsky turned taking her eye off of SAB for the first time as she listened into the phone then headed for the television. Before she could reach it SAB grabbed her by her arm, his grip was tight. Agent Brinsky reflexes kicked in, she spun counter clock wise away from SAB slamming her elbow into his wrist, it was some kind of Aikido move freeing her arm.

"Are you crazy grabbing me like that?" She scorned as she stood with parted legs and feet planted as if she was ready for anything.

"The phone, give me the phone," He demanded.

Brinsky stood up in a relaxed posture and shoved the display screen in SAB's paranoid face, it read call ended 00:07.

"He ended the call after seven seconds, just long enough to give us a warning." She said storming pass SAB heading towards the television for the second time.

It was official she thought as the television blared on and a pyramid of faces was displayed with SAB's face on the second level of the pyramid. Just like that the Brooklyn born and raised agent who served his country since his Boy Scott years was now officially labeled a Most Wanted and a coconspirator in practically every terrorist act since 9-11 without even a day in court.

Agent Brinsky turned and looked at SAB as he listened to the broadcast. The news reporter sounded like she was reading one of Cortexes propaganda reports that almost convinced SAB that Arif Salaam was a terrorist and belonged on the most wanted list.

The only thing different, it was Christopher Black a.k.a. Khalif Ibn Sajud that was now being added to the list.

"His whereabouts are unknown, but the Bureau is yet to confirm if he was killed in yesterday's explosion in Long Island that the terrorist he aided is responsible for."

"In more tragic news, the 19 year old who was shot by police officers earlier today has died. David Squalls family and church are outraged and taking it to the street over the fact the police responsible for Squalls death worked at the same precinct that killed Sean Dell a few years ago. Community activist-"

"The verdict is in." Agent Brinsky surmised as she turned off the television set and faced SAB "They think you're dead."

Brinsky said the verdict was in, hardly and far from it. Special Agent Christopher Black was not dead neither was the truth. "I take it you rode along to help?" SAB asked Brinsky dismissing the news report.

"Yeah, something like that." Brinsky remarked inquisitively.

"How about you start by grabbing us some wheels while I figure out my next move?"

"How about you tell me what happened last night in long Island so I can go in whole hearted on this. I mean, the more I know the more I can help."

"You're right." SAB said as he flipped open the case his father left behind. "On the drive back I'll brief you." SAB insisted.

"Sounds like a plan," Brinsky agreed as she started towards the door then stopped in her tracks after observing the contents of the suit case. "What did your father do for a living? That stuff looks like something out of an espionage movie. How did your father come up with all that in such short notice?" Brinsky asked as her eyes inspected the seal on the passport, the model of the phone that wasn't commercial, the two guns, extra magazines and a silencer. A stack of money covered some documents. From where she stood she couldn't see the other gadgets. Then she thought about what Mr. Black Sr. said.

"When I heard the disc last night I was going to find this mutual friend of ours and the lady Lillian Dalton. But after hearing the news about you, I figured if they wanted my son I'll give them my son." Agent Brinsky realized that Mr. Black Sr. was really going to after Mr. Richard and Cortex and from the looks of that suit case he was capable.

"He always had this stuff sitting around. As for what he did in what most would call a previous life is not important now. After the service he gave this country he didn't deserve this, we don't deserve this." SAB shook his head as the thought passed over him for the first time that his whole family, him, his mother and father lived to serve this country.

## ANTHONY BREWER

The moment Agent Brinsky walked out the door to go find some transportation SAB grabbed the suit case, took the keys off the table and was on his way without her. The last thing he needed was a judgmental, good willed rookie on his heels slowing him down.

Plus rookies were usually the ones that caught the first bullet. Especially since he wasn't going to be playing by any rules she ever heard of.

He left the cabin door open so she could get back in when she returned. He went around the back of the cabin where he hoped to find the SUV that matched the keys he was holding. He found the truck, along with Agent Brinsky sitting in the passenger seat. Though SAB was surprised, he stepped to the truck like he expected her to be in it.

"I take it you figured out your next move?" she asked.

"Yup!" SAB replied as he climbed into the truck. "I'm taking you back to headquarters. I need somebody there to keep me posted."

## CHAPTER FIFTEEN

**Kawi has been watching from a block off** through his binoculars as customers come and go from the restaurant. Kawi looked to the rear where a woman patiently sat sipping a cup of tea since he arrived 35 minutes ago.

Kawi didn't know who she was, but since she sat at the table in the rear next to the fire extinguisher where he was told to sit and make contact, she must have been waiting for him.

"Do you mind if I sit?"

"Only if you buy me lunch." She said with an accent as she studied Kawi's brown eyes.

"I am willing to buy you more than lunch, yes." Kawi replied returning a half smile then felt subconscious about adding the 'yes' hoping she didn't think he was trying to slight her for her accent.

Amused by Kawi she gave him a full smile as she gently nodded her head. Kawi sat without taking his eyes off her. The woman was in her mid to upper twenties and very attractive, Kawi didn't expect that.

"You didn't expect a woman?" she asked placing a bag on the table. "If a man asked you to take off all your clothes, would you?" she slid a gym bag across the table to him. "Everything, please," She insisted pointing to a sign that read restroom.

The bag contained a sweat suit and sneakers. Kawi took that bag along with the one he brought with him into the bathroom. When Kawi stepped out the bathroom she was standing in front of it waiting. She placed her finger over his lips and pushed him back into the bathroom.

Her action alarmed him and at the same time reminded him of the nature of his business. He quickly unzipped his bag revealing an H&K MP5 that was surrounded by bank rolled bundles of twenties, fifties and hundred's.

She timidly leaned in and whispered into his ear. "You don't need that, we have plenty of those for you." She pulled back, made eye contact with Kawi and started from the beginning with the half smile "Yes!" she added in a strong accent to mock him.

"Yes." Kawi replied weakly feigning her accent to amuse her once more.

She quickly grabbed the MP5 out the bag and dropped it in a tall metal trash can along with his bag of personal belongings. She then closed the can, locked it and ran her gadget over Kawi and his bag once more and gave him a full smile when the gadget failed to beep.

Kawi followed her out of the back of the Pizza shop to where a white seatless, windowless moving van sat. After fifteen to twenty minutes of bouncing around in the back of the van they reached their destination. Where, Kawi had no clue beyond the obvious once he stepped out the van and seen it was a warehouse.

A vacant warehouse he first thought, until a freight elevator carried him to the third floor that looked like a shopping department or a display of a manufacturer of weapons and apparel, now Kawi really smiled.

"Meet my uncle. Since I like you, you can call him uncle, yes?" She smiled and walked away leaving Kawi with the man referred to as uncle. *'I like you too!'* Kawi thought to himself as he made a point of not watching her shapely body walk away. Without saying a word Kawi extended his hand giving uncle a firm hand shake, then handed him the bag.

"Thank you," Uncle said taking the duffel bag. He bounced the bag in the air as if he was weighing it and could tell him the exact amount in the bag. "Seem to be a lot of money here. There are a lot of things here that will interest you, so you may be here a while. If you care for something to eat or drink please let him know." Uncle gestured with his head.

Kawi turned to his right to see a man standing next to him. 'Unbelievable!' Kawi thought to himself thinking these people were on top of their game or he was slipping.

What was more unbelievable was the selection of artillery he had to choose from. Kawi's Uncle Jimmy has been doing business off and on with the man called Uncle for the last decade or so. Uncle Jimmy's side hustle was selling fire arms until he fell ill and lost his battle with an incurable case of cancer and decided to pass on his connect to his nephew.

There was enough apparel for it to be a section of its own. Then there was the small side arms and other hand held gadgets. The third section had everything from machine guns, Mack 90's, Calicos to rocket launchers. An hour into Kawi's shopping spree Uncle appeared.

"I counted $65,000 you can order things that are not here."

"I am grateful, but what you have here will suffice. In fact my list is complete and I already instructed your brother of my needs. How will you arrange transportation?"

"All you have to do is tell me when and where you would like it delivered."

*'Clearly this was the difference between having money and a good connect,'* Kawi thought as he was being driven back to the pizza shop. He retrieved his clothes, got dressed and wasted no time getting back, he had a delivery coming.

"As salaamu alaikum," Kawi said jovially greeting everyone as he entered Hussein's house a little more chipper than usual. The return greetings were not as full and warm as his, which made him concerned. Hussein never gave half baked salaams, his greetings were always full with warmth and you knew he meant 'Peace be unto you' when he said it unless something was wrong.

Kawi's demeanor changed instantly sensing something awry. He quickly turned to Sandi who sat expressionless. Then his eyes searched over Hassan, Idris then he went back to Hussein. "Where is my cousin?" Kawi asked.

"He tried to call you before he left, you must have turned your phone off," Idris advised as he stood to approach Kawi.

"Yeah, they took every precaution not to be followed or tracked including stripping me down to my birthday suit. Which reminds me we have a shipment of very choice equipment on the way. Now where is Al Amin?" Kawi asked for a second time.

"He got a call two hours ago. It's your brother, he got shot." Idris said regretting that was not the first thing he said when Kawi returned.

"He's in the hospital. Your family is there and Al Amin went to find out as much information as possible before anyone jumped to any conclusions." Hussein said chiming in trying to keep Kawi calm.

Kawi stood there stunned. It was unconceivable that his little church boy brother got shot. Kawi wasn't upset because he really couldn't believe it, it didn't register.

Everybody in Kawi's house was Muslim except his little brother Daud. His mother came from a Christian home, she eventually embraced Islam then she had Daud who was adverse to Islam and its teachings since he thought he knew the difference. He learned that Daud translated to David as in the Apostle David and that became the only name he would answer to.

"You serious? What somebody tried to steal the church offering and little David tried to slay Goliath." Kawi said with a smirk but his tense body language showed different from the fake smile he's been practicing with the pretty girl from the pizza shop. It was obvious he was fighting not to believe his little brother was shot.

The room fell quiet when Idris cell phone rang. Everyone looked on full of nerves because they all knew the call was about Daud. As much as Kawi tried to fight it he also knew.

"Innal lalahi wa innal lalahi rajaun." Idris said as his head dropped and he shoved the phone into his pocket. Idris slowly raised his head and looked at Kawi.

Kawi's eyes were heavy on the verge of flooding, *'But he couldn't be, he was a child'*. "Aaaaahhhhh!" Kawi screamed as tears poured from his eyes "No not David!" he shouted as he dropped to his knees.

Hassan, Hussein, Idris, not even Al Amin never seen him like this before, so over course they didn't know what to say or how to react since Kawi has always been the hardest amongst them.

The door opened, it was Al Amin seeing his cousin on his knees struggling to gather his composure. Al Amin only wished he didn't take it so hard because what angered him made him kill. What will happen now that he shed tears for his younger brother?

Kawi clambered to his feet and turned to his cousin with tears in his eyes. "I am sorry." Al Amin offered as he embraced his cousin. "Don't be." Kawi replied with a husky voice. "He lived a sinless life. Allah will be merciful for his way of trying to understand religion. So there is no need to be sorry for my little brother, be sorry for whoever shot him." Kawi told Al Amin then turned to look at the others.

## CHAPTER SIXTEEN

**SAB pulled up in front of 225 Cadman Plaza** and handed Agent Brinsky the Pandora report. "This is your stop." Brinsky looked at SAB then at the report in his hand. "What am I suppose to do with that?"

"You're the rookie with big ideas. I already told you what you had to do, you figure out how to do it." SAB shoved the report in her lap as she looked around. Brinsky didn't move she just sat there. SAB reached over her and opened her door. "You said you wanted to help, start by getting out and doing what we talked about," SAB said pointing at the police approaching them.

Seeing the police stopped her from saying what she has been building up to say the whole ride, something she thought he needed to know. Abruptly she jumped out the truck literally into the arms of the approaching police officers dropping the report like a cluts. When she and the officer looked up for the truck she came in, her ride was gone.

"Well well well, we have a celebrity guess." Agent McCarthy announced. Simms and Jenkins looked up as Agent Brinsky entered the office. Her blue eyes bounced off the faces of her coworkers as she paused inside the doorway then continued towards McCarthy. "BLAM" was the sound of the Pandora report falling on McCarthy's desk. "This will make me a celebrity." She proclaimed.

"But why did you call me a celebrity?" She asked out of curiosity.

"Since you stormed out this morning I must have taken about six messages for you," Simms answered.

"At that point we realized no one wanted to speak to us, so we figured why answer the phone," Jenkins said.

"So we decided to do like he said." Simms gestured to McCarthy "Wait for the celebrity."

Six messages, Brinsky sprinted over to her desk. She was the rookie no one even knew she was in the Bureau much less a number at Cadman Plaza where she could be reached.

McCarthy sat there jumping from page to page spot reading excerpts, anything in parenthesis and bold lettering. After a few minutes of that he had to stop and look at the front page to see what he was reading and who wrote it.

McCarthy knew SAB so he knew before the polls closed SAB would get something to his team to give them a heads up. The problem was, the report didn't make any sense and it had nothing to do with him nor said anything to vindicate him. McCarthy didn't read the whole report but nothing he read had anything to do with anything that transpired in New York or even America for the last couple of weeks.

"So what's the verdict chief?" Simms asked when he seen McCarthy look up like he was missing something. McCarthy got up, placed the report on Simms desk then turned to Agent Brinsky who was just finishing her second call and was about to make her third.

"Woe there before you do that." McCarthy said approaching cautiously knowing as SAB did that Brinsky was a bit on the defensive side.

Agent Brinsky sat upright and her facial expression changed from the poised celebrity to the cautious agent as she read the sobering look on McCarthy's face. His eyes beamed into hers. He saw her eyes widen with anticipation as he approached so he threw her a curve ball.

"Agent Brinsky did you know federal agents were actually involved in the Oklahoma City bombing?"

"What do you mean involved?" she shot back to see what he was implying.

"Involved like the planning of and conspiring to."

From the look on her face this was news and class was now is session. Not only for Brinsky, Simms, and Jenkins alike, they were not in the Bureau in 1995. After the explosion and shit hit the fan in Oklahoma, that same shit came rolling down hill on the entire special opt teams, informants and undercover agents working that case. Some were pulled off the case and some were even charged when the finger pointing commenced.

"My whole team was pulled from New York and sent out there. At the time I was still learning the ropes, so I learned some hard lessons fast. In a bureaucracy as big as ours they don't have a problem passing the buck. You don't want to know what happened to the agents who got caught up in that case. In this case the buck stops here."

"I hear you, understand you, but the buck will not stop here." Brinsky wanted to end that statement by saying she promised them that, but she didn't want to get ahead of herself. Now it was clear she knew something they didn't and they were right back to where they were when she walked through the door wanting answers. McCarthy asked her one simple question, "What's going on?"

Brinsky dropped her head and began shuffling the small pieces of paper the messages were on. "Whoever labeled him a terrorist is in the Bureau," she began then slowly looked up.

"SAB is going is to find him and expose him because that same person is likely to be the same person who helped cover up his mother's murder. I don't know what he's going to do."

Brinsky looked around the room. "But I do know those people will get it the worse," She said pointing and they all turned to see what at. They looked at the report Simms was holding.

"Hey McCarthy guess who wrote this?" Simms asked with the daring game face he often used. McCarthy seen a name on the cover but it didn't ring a bell, but it did. Simms saw the spark in McCarthy's eyes. "That's right, the poor guy Doyle and O' Patrick slugged. According to this he was some kind of journalist spilling the beans on somebody at the top of the food chain."

"And the other name on it?" McCarthy asked. To that Simms could only repeat what he heard on the news. It was Brinsky who chipped in from there, starting with the night Walton and Jenkins had to stop their tail so she and SAB could attend a meeting with the journalist Pandora without the prying eyes of Cortex.

**TERRORIST IN BROOKLYN**

Then finally Brinsky gave them the flip side of the coin. She told them everything that happened since Sandi appeared on the scene up until 15 minutes ago when SAB dropped her off. After she spilled her guts she posed a question to McCarthy, Simms, Jenkins and Walton that would ultimately decide where the buck would stop.

"How could justice be served in the more traditional manner, without SAB going on a killing spree?"

## CHAPTER SEVENTEEN

"**Yes, how can I help you?**" the desk Sergeant asked looking up from a pile of papers.

"Are you Sergeant Lancy? I was told he had desk duty and would be easy to find," The man assumed.

"Desk duty doesn't mean easy to find. What's this about?" The desk Sergeant asked seeming frustrated suddenly.

The man pulled out a piece of paper out of nowhere. "I am a process server. I serve and I go, don't stick a plunger up my ass. Unless you want to interfere with the Mayor's office and get served yourself." The server paused and waited for an answer.

"Get the fuck out my face, Lancy's in the back." The desk Sergeant growled then went back to his pile of papers.

"I thought so!" The server replied as he took his hand out his pocket and threw something in the trash.

The server went unnoticed as he made his way around the far end of the precinct, then to the desk in the rear where Sergeant Lancy sat in a debate with two Detectives. Today's topic was about, whether O.J. Simpson sentence for robbery was a bit extreme or did it make up for him not doing time for allegedly killing his wife.

"I still say divorcing her would have been cheaper and much easier, especially when you catch her braking marriage vows with the help." A passing Detective chimed in.

"What's up with these fucking football players anyway? One is hanging dogs, another is shooting himself and the old guy is what, what he said at sentencing, he was trying to steal his stuff back and he was only sorry he used a gun. For Christ sake already these guys."

"Excuse me gentlemen I hate to interrupt, Sergeant Lancy?"

The balding Detective with the tweed sport coat, who was leaning back with his feet up like he didn't have a care in the world, looked up acknowledging his name and rank. "What do you want?"

"Are you Sergeant Lancy?"

"I might be who are you?"

The process server pulled out a different piece of paper than the one he showed the desk Sergeant, he cleared his throat and began to read it. "Mr. Lancy, Sergeant at the 87th Precinct Crime Division, are now served by the community, family and friends of and for David Squall." The server handed Sergeant Lancy the paper he was holding.

"What the hell is this?" Lancy demanded as he threw his feet off the desk slamming them on the floor as he stood with fury tossing the paper.

The Detective next to him snatched the paper out of the air. He read the words just heard recited then squinted his eyes as he tried to read the caption on the news paper clipping that seemed to be pasted to the page. It was a clipping from the Amsterdam News of David Squalls body sprawled out in a puddle of blood.

In the rear of the photo he could see the cross from the church he was killed in front of. The caption read "Another youth shot down by the cops paid to protect him." A quote taken from the mother of Sean Dell who was also shot down in cold blood by a cop from the 87th Precinct.

"I said what the hell is this?" Sergeant Lancy roared looking as if he was going to leap over the desk at the server who turned to walk away. The server turned away quickly, all you could see was the tail of his full length black leather gliding in the air as if it was his cape.

The server who was now the center of attention stopped in his tracks and spun full circle like he forgot something. At the sight of two modified 45. Caliber weapons in his hand with extended clips hanging from the bottom of it, it seemed like the whole precinct leaped up at once.

Before Sergeant Lancy who was already standing could unholster his weapon, Jimmy Squalls guns were already locked on his target. "This is for the little guy!" Jimmy grimaced as he simultaneously squeezed the triggers of his 45's. The impact of both bullets hitting Sergeant Lancy had the effect of a 50 caliber removing the top of the Sergeant's head.

A series of slugs hit Jimmy in the back only knocking him forward, closer to the targets before him. The piece of paper was still air bound as the bullets pierced through it and into the Detective that dropped it to reach for his weapon.

Not even Jimmy's bullet proof coat could withstand the salvo of close range hits. Police screamed out as they were hit, others went for cover either to get a better shot or to wait for the mad gunman to empty his clips.

There was one shot the rang out louder than the rest, it was the single shot to the side of Jimmy's head. As soon as it hit, the officer that delivered the lucky shot jumped out "I got em!" he declared.

The room closed in, a few officers took shots at Jimmy's already dead body as they approached. Only if they knew he was already dead before that from the cancer that was untreatable they would have shot him a couple more times.

"BOOM" "BOOM" "BOOM" three discharges went off around the perimeter of the precinct where Jimmy dropped them before he made it to Sergeant Lancy's desk. Most of the officer's who closed in towards the center of the room where David's uncle laid was safe but still they ducked for cover until they realized it was only smoke bombs.

As the smoke cleared and danger was no longer immanent they began to emerge from underneath desk, behind file cabinets or whatever form of cover they took hoping it would save them.

"What the fuck?" One cop shouted after spotting three figures standing in the entrance of the precinct wearing mask and long black trench coats carrying AK 47 assault rifles.

The slow menacing steps they took through the dissipating smoke was enough notice that these men were not there to help. They never hesitated to shoot first and ask questions later and now was no time to change that policy. The police opened fire on their targets without hesitation.

The three men seemed to be in no hurry to return fire as some slugs embedded in the bullet proof coats and others bounced off.

ANTHONY BREWER

All three men bent their knees, hugged their weapons close to their bodies and fired in a slow concentrated motion from right to left, then from side to side of the precinct.

The wave of bullets swept across the station ripping through all it came in contact with. After one sweeping motion the men paused and waited before sweeping again. This time one man shot high and another shot low and the third man stayed focused straight ahead, they wanted everyone even those who played possum.

Content they accomplished what they set out to do the three men left taking the body of Jimmy Squall with them.

## CHAPTER EIGHTEEN

**After SAB dropped Agent Brinsky off** at Cadman Plaza he set out on his mission. Do to last night's fiasco he knew for a fact Sandi was with Imam Ibraheem's son Idris. Now all he had to do was find Idris. For Special Agent Black that would be a problem, for Khalif Ibn Sajud it should be a simple task.

Sajud reasoned with himself that if he brought in Sandi, that would not only prove he wasn't working with them, it would restore his standing in the Bureau despite the attempts to discredit him and make him look like a terrorist. Then he could more effectively attend to his personal agenda without undo recourse.

Call it disguise or religious adornment, but Sajud knew no one would recognize him in a Jalibir and kufi. With his humble and pious character it would be easy for him to blend into any community undetected.

Sajud knew Imam Ibraheem or someone at the Mosque knew where Idris was or how to contact him. Regardless how dead set the Imam appeared to be against his son for partaking in such activities, he was still his son which made Idris the son of the entire community.

Sajud circled the block where the Imams Mosque was. He was confident there were at least two separate surveillance teams watching the Mosque. He was just as confident he would have no problems getting in because he knew the protocol. No one was going to expose the opt because they thought they seen someone who looked like Special Agent Black dressed in Muslim clothes.

Sajud sat patiently waiting for his cue and he heard it, the call to prayer for the evening salat. Sajud got out of his truck and mixed in with those who were answering the call.

He made it into the mosque without incident and followed the ritual movement from the making of ablution to finding a spot on the floor to where he made two units of prayer in respect to the Mosque as he waited for the main prayer to begin.

Sajud was a bit nervous because he never performed a congregation prayer in a mosque before. Maybe once or twice as a small child but that didn't count because he prayed amongst children and they usually played while they prayed.

The nervousness resided at the second call to prayer and they all stood for prayer in a group. It was pretty much the same thing he did when he prayed alone. Despite how much he concealed his religious beliefs, he never failed in his religious obligations.

The prayer ended quickly and most of the people left the Mosque just as fast as they came to it. He didn't want to be left alone and stick out so he had to move quickly. It was hard to get someone's attention long enough to go beyond salutations since no one knew him. Regardless how kind and cordial everyone seemed, he wasn't just going to jump out there asking questions. He was still in Brooklyn and in Brooklyn he already learned they dumped the dead bodies of informants in abandoned parks.

As he stood he felt someone coming behind him. He quickly glanced over his shoulder. It was one of the men from Mosque security. Sajud looked ahead trying to avoid eye contact but it was inevitable, the man grabbed Sajud by the shoulder.

"Should I call you agent?" the man asked.

Sajud spun around to face his fear. Sajud recognized Abdul from the raid with Agent Tinsely. Sajud brushed the man's hand off his shoulder, "If you know my name is Sajud that's what you call me."

The man frowned his face and pushed his way pass Sajud. "The Imam wants to see you, now."

Sajud looked at the two men standing in the rear of the Mosque looking on. He could tell from their facial expressions they too were security and was waiting for something to go down, Sajud followed his escort.

Instead of the man turning right where Sajud knew the Imams office to be he turned left then headed down a flight of steps. Now Sajud became concerned and stopped at the top of the steps. He took a deep breath and the face of the dead agent they found in the park came to mind as clear as if he was still standing over the body.

Without any hesitation Sajud darted down the steps behind the man dismissing his concerns. The fact remained he was still Muslim and he was amongst Muslims. Only in the Middle East did Muslims kill Muslims. That was not an issue in Brooklyn amongst African American Muslims.

The tall somewhat muscular brother led Sajud down the first flight of steps then into the basement. The basement was dark with the exception of a bright light coming from a room at the end of the lengthy basement, Sajud followed.

"I've been waiting to ask you Mr. Double Agent, who are working for on this visit?" The Imam asked upon seeing Sajud as he shuffled boxes around in a storage area.

"How about triple agent because I am working for me, myself and I, and we all have an agenda."

The Imam smirked as he looked over at Sajud expecting that much to be true after what he heard on the news. "If that's the case I have a message for you," The Imam informed Sajud as he waved off the Mosque security.

Sajud stood there watching the Imam push the sliding door closed wondering who this message could be from or was he going to make a confessional that he also knew his mother.

"Tell me what it is you want most?" The Imam asked as he left the sliding door he just closed and walked to the opposite side of the room and continued to remove boxes from the pile he was working on when Sajud entered the room. He then pushed a piece of sheet rock to the side revealing another sliding door.

"It's not as simple as that," Sajud replied to the Imam's question.

"Actually it is," The Imam shouted while struggling with the sliding door that hasn't been moved in years. "You can help me with this door or we will have the time for you to tell me why my question is so complicated." Sajud raised three fingers as he took his position on the door and the Imam began counting "One, two, three." They pushed hard and the door did not budge until the second try it opened than closed with one simple push.

Sajud followed the Imam through a passage way that use to be a coal room for the two adjacent buildings. They went through the boiler room and came out the basement around the corner from the Mosque undetected. There the Imam had his car parked only a few feet away from the exit as if he had the whole thing planned.

*'But how could he have been part of this plan if they didn't know I was coming to the Mosque in the first place.'* Sajud thought to himself as he tried to figure out where the Imam was taking him. A smile crept on his face of all the questions Agent Brinsky would be asking at that very moment.

"Do you mind?" Sajud asked reaching for the ON button of the car radio. The Imam glanced over at Sajud and saw only his calm exterior and expressionless face. "You read my mind." The Imam replied taking note of how Sajud was surfing stations looking to avoid news reports. "It's good to stay abreast of what's going on," The Imam warned.

"Oh really! That's a mouthful coming from you." Sajud replied referring to the Imam not knowing about Idris and Sandi.

"That's old news, you need to catch up." The Imam retorted putting the news on. There was no mention of Sandi and the explosion or of a rogue agent wanted for treason. Those stories were overshadowed by reports of a shooting at a police station in Brooklyn.

"Then bring me up to speed on what's current in the news Mr. Ibraheem." Sajud Suggested.

"In a matter of minutes you can do something that can take a life time to undo."

"Okay." Sajud nodded appreciatively of the wisdom the Imam imparted.

"In your case-" The Imam continued as he swerved through traffic. "There is something's you have not done that could take you a lifetime to even know that you have to do. Hence the big question everyone has, why am I here? Then suddenly something dramatic or life altering happens and what they knew as life changed. NOW-" The Imam emphasized as he pulled over and looked at Sajud "do you go backwards or forward. Do you go back to what you knew or embrace that thing that can answer the big question who am I and why am I here.

Luckily this whole thing blew up in your face because now you're presented with the opportunity that can answer your big question. Most people are content, they do what they know how to do and are used to doing.

Don't try and tell them they are living in the past or going backwards. Just know they'll never take that step forward or get answers to their big questions."

There were no big questions for Sajud or SAB, only one agenda, revenge. Only meaning one thing to Sajud, going forward and letting the cards fall where they may. "And you're telling me all this because?" Sajud asked.

"Right now you need a life line, something to prove you are not that traitor they say you are. I know this as I knew you would come here to find that life line. I am going to give you that line and in return I need something from you."

Sajud turned and looked at Imam Ibraheem expecting his list of demands be more clearly stated. And more importantly Sajud wanted to know what that life line was. The life line was Idris.

"Why your son, why not give me Sandi?"

"The life, honor and property of a Muslim is sacred. I cannot give you anyone. If my son did not come forth on his own will to clear my name and our community of wrong doing I would have nothing to give you."

"What is it you ask of me?"

"As my son will tell you, me, my wife and younger son had no knowledge nor took part in anything of his doing. I ask you to promise that we are treated accordingly and our community is not harassed."

That was a promise he should be able to give to anyone innocent man of wrong doing and the Imam hasn't shown anything to the contrary thus far. Sajud promised using the operative term "IF" he was restored back to his position of authority he would uphold such promise.

The "IF" relied on more than Sajud could conceive being possible unless the Imam knew something Sajud didn't. The Imam pointed to the building he parked in front of. In the third floor window a man looked down and watched them. Sajud immediately recognized the man from a photo, it was Idris.

Idris watched his father exit the car from the window he stood in and spoke on the phone as he watched traffic. His last words before he disconnected were informing the other party that the FBI man was in the building and that he wished them success.

Sajud followed Imam Ibraheem up three flights of steps and into Idris's apartment. He entered cautiously after looking down at Idris who only reached shoulder level to him. Idris greeted his father in the doorway but didn't allow him any further. He thanked him and asked him to make Dua for them, then sent his father on his way.

Sajud studied Idris and wondered if he was the man that attacked the two NYPD officers and the federal agents at Sandi's house, during the abduction if Sandi's niece and nephew. Sajud had to know so he asked, that was his first question and Idris affirmed. Now Sajud knew how well Idris could handle himself and how audacious he was.

As soon as the Imam left Idris locked the door and the first thought that came to SAB's mind was *'This is exactly how they would love to catch me with my alleged coconspirator.'* That was not a good look for Sajud or Special Agent Black.

"Where is Sandi?" Sajud asked as a precursor to getting the ball rolling and finding out why he was there. Idris didn't answer, he just stood there looking at Sajud while he mentally flipped through a rolodex of preconceived notions of how Sajud the Muslim slash FBI agent would look, act, speak, dress and the list went on.

"As salaamu alaikum partner." Idris offered in the place of an answer to Sajud's question to subside the agitation Idris seen growing in Sajud's face.

"Wa laikum, and I'm not your partner."

"Then you're my enemy?"

"Enemy is a strong word. But what I will say is if I had a job, we would have a problem," Sajud warned.

"How about I get you your job back, then we can be brothers in faith and work on-"

Sajud raised his hand stopping Idris. "Your quick to speak and I am sure beyond measure."

"So you're saying then that you don't want your job back."

"No, I'm saying-"

"No! It's what I'm saying that counts." Idris said cutting Sajud off.

*'Finally!'* Sajud thought as he paused and waited for the reason he was brought there. The first words out of Idris mouth about giving Sajud more than he came for went over his head. And it made absolutely no sense when Idris said something about turning himself in.

Sajud couldn't believe what he was hearing and didn't have time to think about what possessed this man to believe that anyone wanted him, much less in Sandi's place. Sajud was there for five minutes which meant he was there for five minutes too long. He brushed pass Idris who was standing in the corridor leading to the door, Sajud went to make his exit.

"The weapon of choice was an AST4 anti tank missile that killed the Supreme Court judge." Idris informed Sajud as he approached the door. "You want to know why that was done or why I am turning myself in." Idris asked.

"Why do you think turning yourself in would make a difference?"

"It's complicated but it will better serve the both of us if I told you-" Idris glanced at his watch, "That in less than an hour someone from that same circle will also be sent back to their maker and I need to be in custody before it happens."

Sajud looked at Idris like he lost his mind and for that reason alone he called Agent Brinsky's phone that he knew would be tapped and asked her if she knew of any specifics about a dead judge. She told him it was a missile attack in the heart of the judicial district confirming what Idris told him. Before she could get into her million questions Sajud hung up on her. "We have to go, now." Sajud demanded.

"Where we headed partner?" Idris inquired after snatching his bag off the table and following Sajud to the door.

"Out of this death trap and the partner thing doesn't fit you," Sajud rebuked as he drew his side arm before opening the door. He placed the FBI badge around his neck, turned back and glanced at Idris as a warning then yanked the door open and shot the first person he saw. SAB shot an African American male, late 20's, clean cut with slacks wearing Rockport shoes and a Columbia wind breaker.

"Are you crazy?" Idris screamed as he went to grab Sajud. Before he could get to him, Sajud let off another shot hitting another man coming down the steps. This one came rolling down the steps and fell flat in front of Idris.

The fact that he was white and he had a government issued H & K in his hand was enough for Idris to realize what time it was.

## TERRORIST IN BROOKLYN

Now Idris didn't believe his eyes *'Did Sajud just body two government agents?'* he thought as he picked up the government issued .45.

Before he could further entertain the thought he was interrupted by a barrage of gun fire. Without batting an eye Idris stepped to the top of the steps while he returned fire. Sajud let off two shots hitting the man to Idris's immediate right on his way up. Idris would have seen him if he didn't go flying down the stairs like he was in a John Woo movie.

"Up, up." Sajud hollered as he changed directions to avoid where he knew their opposition would be coming from. As fast as they could, Sajud and Idris ran to the roof. From the lack of resistance he knew they just arrived the very moment Sajud realized they had to move out. The first two he laid out had to be scouts which meant they weren't trapped and they had a small advantage.

As soon as he hit the roof they ran across from one roof to another, until they crossed at least seven buildings putting them at the end of the block. They climbed down the back of a building on its fire escape, then shot across the court yard to an adjoining court yard, entered another building through the back and came out the front of another building on a different block all together.

Sajud moved like he lived in the ghetto all his life. Idris stayed on his heals watching every move almost admiring every step Sajud took towards their escape. It wasn't that Idris couldn't get away on his own, it was more about being led by the trained FBI agent who was his older Muslim brother in faith.

As soon as Sajud hit the street, his eye scanned the dark but well occupied streets for anything that looked out of place. Though people were standing around, it seemed normal for that time of night in that neighborhood. He glanced at his watch then with hurried steps approached two men getting out of a white 750 series BMW.

"FBI, I need to commandeer this vehicle." He insisted waving his badge he had hanging around his neck. He grabbed the keys out of the driver's hand not giving him an option or before he could detest.

"Na man you can't take my car," The man said as he stepped up trying to take his keys back. "Plus how the hell I know you guys are no fucking fake ass police in the first place."

Which was a legitimate question considering how Sajud and Idris was dressed in what looked like a dress over jeans. Sajud raised his jalibir to get access to his back pocket, displaying the gun he had in his belt in the same motion to clam the man down. Sajud handed the man his card he took out of his wallet. "You'll get your car back by morning the latest, bill it to the war on terrorism." Sajud said pushing the man aside.

"Last chance you want custody?" Sajud asked as they climbed into the BMW.

"It's the only way or I will be looked upon as a terrorist."

"You are a terrorist, but we are not going there. My question is what makes you think they will let you or me for that matter waltz you up in there because I got you in cuffs? And clear my name In doing so!" Sajud added.

"Trust me!" Idris said giving Sajud a nod of confidence.

Sajud looked at Idris like he was crazy. He had to be if he thought just on his two words "Trust me!" they were going anywhere. Sajud pulled into a municipal parking lot he seen. He took a ticket and parked on the second level by the railing over the front entrance of which they came so they could watch traffic.

Idris's cavalier attitude was typical of most African Americans who partook in illegal activities without fully appraising the repercussions of their actions. Which was evident here when the FBI, NYPD and God knows how many mercenaries Cortex had on their payroll searching for them.

"I can get you reinstated," Idris offered. "I get you reinstated, then I have someone on the inside to look after my best interest."

"What makes you think I care about your best interest. You're a terrorist responsible for the deaths of FBI and local police. My sense of duty dictates that you are put away, for life."

"Would that same sense of duty allocate fair treatment and due process while you're trying to put me away for life?"

"I will not be the one trying you, but I suppose once the cameras get turned on-"

"That's right, once I walk through the door with you I will get every camera from here to Europe." Idris said interrupting to make his point.

"If all you want to do is take responsibility for your actions so nothing falls on your father and his community, you don't need cameras and a parade?" Sajud questioned Idris trying to pry

ANTHONY BREWER

further since it was obvious he was up to something much more then saving his father.

Idris's face frowned at the prospect that Sajud was suggesting he was doing this for notoriety. *'You're worrying about your ass in total disregard for what is going on out here in this jungle and you have the nerve to insinuate shit.'* Is what Idris wanted to say. "First I will tell you I am not a terrorist, which is why I need the cameras so I can make it known. And you're wrong I am not just doing this for my father."

"Why then?"

Idris looked at the traffic below, "The last couple of weeks I have done things-." Idris paused and slowly turned his head towards Sajud and made eye contact "That I often thought about but never imagined doing." Idris stopped again, this time he looked at his watch.

"What made you decide to be FBI and serve your country?" Idris asked. Seeing Sajud was not quick to reply to the personal question, "Quid pro quo?" Idris insisted.

Sajud looked at Idris who was at least five years his junior. What made Sajud think of Idris's age was the questioning look on his face. Not so much Sajud's questions, but something Idris questioned in himself.

"I am somewhere between wanting to serve my country and wanting a little power for myself." Sajud began. "What made you decide to get involved in terrorist activity?" Sajud asked.

"I am more a reactionary hinging on revolutionary. Have you ever heard the expression one man's terrorist is another man's freedom fighter. But never can you call me a terrorist, your government is the real terrorist. Have you ever killed a Muslim in the line of duty?"

Sajud shook his head. "No, not to my knowledge. Since I suppose to be your coconspirator, you want to tell me to what?"

"Could you?" Idris asked looking straight ahead into the traffic below. Sajud overlooked the fact he didn't answer his question.

"Like your father said, by Allah the life, honor and property of a Muslim is sacred." Sajud answered thinking about Arif Salaam knowing that if Doyle and O' Patrick didn't kill Arif he would have handled their situation differently and more than likely they would still be alive.

"I take it you know about the dead informant we left in the park?" Idris asked. Sajud replied with three nods of the head. "And about the building in Long Island?"

"I was buried under it."

Idris stopped there these were the only things that could be linked to Sajud by way of Sandi. There was no need to expose his other ambitions. "What about the Supreme Court Judge, how does that play into all this?" Sajud asked since it appeared Idris wasn't going any further.

"You don't need to know about that because it had nothing to do with Sandi, you or Islam."

"It's all the same, I need the whole picture. They're calling us partners, you're calling us partners. I need to feel like a partner right now!"

## ANTHONY BREWER

"When you're in a room with people and you hear something for the first time, everyone knows from your reaction that that was the first time you heard about it, it proves you're innocence."

"It doesn't prove anything other than maybe how naïve someone was." Sajud shot back. " It was you who asked me to trust you." He continued staring at Idris, "Killing an informant and blowing up a building with several agents already put you over the top. Let's just call this thing we're doing here, bonding."

A smirk appeared on Idris face after he glanced at his watch for the third time. "You remember that Muslim brother from Africa that was shot up in the hallway of his building by police, over 50 rounds were fired. He was unarmed they ruled it all in a day's work and acquitted the officers. So it was no surprise when the cops gave Sean Dell the same treatment and we got the same results.

Every time we drag someone into court for killing one of ours, the courts send a loud and clear message back to us saying what Dred Scott and Malcolm X said was true, that we have no human rights they respect." Idris glanced at his watch again. "That was only a small part of our reply or reaction to their actions." Idris taunted. "How does the African American Muslim FBI agent feel about that?"

Sajud's face was blank. How should any African American feel about the neolynching practices of local police, court sytem and their legislators  throughout the 52 states, when it came to people of color.

Sajud was not going to express such feelings to Idris and give credence to anything he did.  "Exactly what action did they take against you that made you react this way or want to revolt all of a sudden?"

'Good question.' Idris thought. One he has been pondering since he passed the point of no return and blew the brains out of that informant in his father's Masjid and all his actions thereafter.

Everything afterwards happened so fast and fell into succession so naturally, it almost made him feel they were doing what they were supposed to be doing or as Kawi referred to it as "Their calling" and what they have been training all these years for, to protect their community.

Their calling was to spread Islam amongst the non believers. At least that's why their parents have been sending them to private schools across the country to learn at the feet of Islamic scholars. The training was only to strengthen them and add balance to spiritual and mental resolve. Using the knowledge they acquired and the training was not for the purpose of starting personal wars and going contrary to the lifestyle of peace they were to espouse.

Idris looked up at Sajud with madness in his eyes. Sajud watched as Idris's eyes glazed over and knew for some reason whatever he was about to say, that sudden crazed look meant it would not be coming from his little bag of tricks but from another place deep inside.

"You said your duty dictates that I be put away for life. Do you know that's how the American majority feels about me before any of this happened, just because I am black and worse because I am Muslim?" Idris asked.

"Man the American majority doesn't even know you it's all in your head."

"I am not talking about me the individual I am talking about the collective body. The black face in America has been hated since the beginning of its existence. Public enemy number one since we were brought to this country in chains to build this place. We are still second rate citizens after the sacrifice, blood and sweat. Guess whose public enemy number one now?" Idris asked and watched Sajud as he waited for an answer.

"I don't know, why don't you tell me."

"Oh you know and knew all along. Your parents knew it too, that's why you hid it and kept your government name. But now they now you're Muslim they automatically call you terrorist. How are you going to react to that, brother?" Idris asked then raised his hand. "Wait, don't answer that. I saw how you reacted when you killed those men back there without blinking an eye or was that revolt?" Idris asked and was stopped by the ringing of his cell phone.

## CHAPTER NINETEEN

**All that has happened McCarthy didn't need a microscope** to see how it all tied back to Special Agent Black. McCarthy had to make a decision that not only would affect his career but more importantly his retirement. All the enmities for full service to his country plus a stepping stone to a cushioned position behind a desk is the standard wish list for anyone retiring.

McCarthy did a brief stint in Vietnam, he was just coming in when they were pulling out of that catastrophe. Still young and eager to serve his country McCarthy served nine years before he was released with honorable discharge and finished his degree in Psychology. It was then that he enlisted in the Federal Bureau of Investigation and since served for fifteen years.

Now that it was all winding down his last decision counted as much as his previous career decisions. Deputy Director Walter Ramen acknowledged McCarthy's future retirement and expressed some of his own concerns about McCarthy's unfortunate situation. Deputy Director Ramen made it clear to McCarthy what he already knew, the Bureau was counting on him in the case against Khalif Ibn Sajud.

As Ramen requested McCarthy contacted Deputy Director Ramen and briefed him. "This will go a long way towards your retirement package." The Deputy instructed after listening to McCarthy's three minute briefing.

"Like you said one hand-"

"Click"

All McCarthy heard was a dial tone. The Deputy heard Special Agent Black was going to clear his name by bringing in Sandi. 'Maybe in that next lifetime they believe in.' The Deputy opined as he dialed Mr. Dercole.

Operation Skeleton has been taking Dercole longer than proposed. He assured Mr. Richard that all loose ends would be nicely tucked away before Mr. Richard announced his political agenda.

What's done in the past to get to the future is justified by success. Only condemned when those actions are evidenced in a political arena where you're looked upon and judged for morality or the lack thereof.

Mr. Richard could continue to flourish as a billion dollar international oil mogul with political ties with several countries. Or, he could choose to take it to the next level as a legitimate politician after he cleaned up his past or got rid of the people who could expose it.

Mr. Dercole's job was a simple one, the process of elimination of a very short list of problems that seemed to be getting longer and longer with a new set of characters like Sandi and his new Sahabahs. Which proved to be even more troublesome since they had a set of skills that the journalist and Cortexes corporate rivals didn't have, guns and the ability to use them.

With Mr. Dercole's two major guns dead and gone, with Special Agent Black on the opposing side, Mr. Richard had to rethink his strategy because at any point he could lose Dercole, which he couldn't phantom.

Mr. Richard needed Dercole his head of security at Cortex. With one of the largest American oil companies to built in a foreign, not to mention most hostile territory in history.

In building one of the largest military bases in Iraq that the U.S. has had in any country thanks to the 800 billion dollars U.S. tax payer's money for the war, the U.S. investors like Mr. Richard was grateful he nor other conglomerates that had the most to gain by the invasion didn't have to sponsor it directly.

Instead they parleyed and waited for the government to go in set up Saddam Hussein with the alleged weapons of mass destruction and everything from Hussein's stash to the control of Iraqi oil was up for grabs.

After the military cleared the way, private contractors like Sheppard equipped with 50,000 plus ex-military, ex-government staff not to mention the freelance Mercenaries which made up another 50,000. The oil barrens were able to ride into Iraq and set up shop without any opposition from an Iraqi government.

There was still opposing factions and militia to deal with which is why Dercole was invaluable. Since the cold war and the employ of men like Bin Laden, Mr. Dercole has been in the trenches of Iraq, Iran and Afghanistan. To say he knew the ropes would be an understatement he controlled them.

With O' Patrick and Doyle gone Mr. Dercole was back and forth in Iraq overseeing the security of Cortexes new empire. A slew of nameless mercenaries were sent to Brooklyn to exterminate that problem. It was a simple search for and destroy mission for Sandi and his crew.

Special Agent Black was going to be treated as a separate problem that had to be handled differently. At some point the mercenaries would tract down Sandi and company but the FBI agent would not be that simple, another approach was called for.

With the call from Deputy Director saying that Special Agent Black was bringing in Sandi, there was a one shot deal to kill two birds with one stone that Cortex couldn't pass up on.

\* \* \* \* \* \* \* \* \*

SAB realized Idris didn't understand how this game was played as he listened to him rage on about the need to turn himself in when no one wanted him. To Cortex Sandi was there patsy enabling them to destroy all their U.S. property and collect billions in insurance money to reinvest in the war for oil. Idris was not in that equation and he couldn't see that because he couldn't see pass his own little world where he wanted justice, for what is still not clear to SAB or in SAB's opinion it still was not clear to Idris neither.

Special Agent Black spoke slowly and clearly explaining the situation to Idris and concluded by telling him, "Contrary to what you think, there is only one way they will handle our situation and that's elimination. Not placating, negotiation or judicial arbitration.

You want to get in front of the camera and tell your story, I want to stop some bad people and close an old account. I can have my team pick you up and bring a news truck. You can clear your father's name and get all the camera coverage you want all the way to the death chamber. Your mission is accomplished and you're out my hair because I am not going anywhere with you," SAB said as he pulled out his phone and started dialing Agent McCarthy.

"I have shit to do that requires me being free and breathing." SAB added as he pushed numbers.

"Alright!" Idris said stopping SAB from making the call. "We all have needs. Mines require also that I am alive and free. I am not trying to become a martyr, at least not now." Idris informed SAB making eye contact with him to get his point across. "I need you, not a team." Idris continued then glanced at his watch. "I told you something was going to happen within the hour, we have seventeen minutes left."

Idris glanced around the parking lot, "The pen is lifted and the ink has dried." Idris said as he pointed to a black Escalade truck. "We needed one of those and it sits right before us. What is meant to happen is meant to happen, it is already written." Idris concluded then told SAB that if he helped him by the end of the ride he would get Sandi.

Idris filled SAB in on his game plan. Though he didn't agree it worked for SAB because it would expose that one person in the Bureau that is working for Cortex and it wouldn't be SAB's word against his because whoever they are they would have to expose themselves to the agency to try and stop SAB from coming in. But

ANTHONY BREWER

in order for this to work SAB had to make sure they knew he was coming and where.

SAB discarded his Muslim garb then called Agent Brinsky and told her he was bringing in Sandi. The plan was tell Brinsky who was his broadcasting system and everyone involved would know their roles. SAB figured whoever was out to stop him would have Brinsky's phone tapped. Deputy Director Ramen was a step ahead, he was in Brinsky's office patiently awaiting SAB's call.

After the last incident at Idris's apartment they fell off the radar. From the call they seen he was still in Brooklyn and from the global positioning of his cell phone it confirmed he was in route to Cadman Plaza just like he said. This simplified a lot of things for the Deputy Director guaranteeing his promotion to Director.

Ramen could see the headlines; "Deputy Director Ramen spearheaded Anti Terrorist Taskforce that saves the city. Known terrorist group and rogue Muslim FBI agent killed in shoot out."

After calling Dercole to finish what Cortex started, the Deputy Director posted his men at Cadman Plaza in the event Mr. Dercole's men couldn't finish the job. This had to end once and for all and the memo Deputy Ramen sent out said nothing about Special Agent Black bringing anyone in, it only stated "The agent responsible for last night's catastrophe was in fact alive and seen in the proximity of Downtown Brooklyn with coconspirators, stop and decease."

As SAB sat at the light waiting for it to change two Chevy Tahoe's pulled up, one on each side of him. They too stopped at the light took a brief glance into SAB's black Escalade then looked ahead waiting for the light to change. The moment the light turned green it meant go to the men in both trucks as they pulled out fully automatic machine guns and started firing at SAB.

The sound of the gun fire was drowned out by the sound of the Escalade tires burning rubber as SAB threw the truck in reverse and slamming on the gas. "BAM" SAB backed into an oncoming car leaving the two Chevy Tahoe's in a cross fire.

Before the cross fire ended SAB was already out of the truck with gun in hand finishing off whoever didn't get caught by the crossfire. He got one truck and Idris finished the other truck load. SAB looked over at Idris while searching for the identification of the driver of the Tahoe.

"Don't waste your time." Idris called out. "They belong to Cortex. These are the same trucks that tried to stop us last night." He said holding up two machine guns he took off the dead bodies. "Ghetto warfare, we pick up we need along the way." He explained.

SAB's attention was drawn by the high beams of oncoming traffic, it was two more trucks. Idris flung SAB one of the machine guns then he took off running straight into the light firing sporadically driver side, passenger side, back and forth until the truck came to a stop.

SAB on the other hand fired two shots killing the driver of the other Tahoe, the truck hit a parked car and went air bound and exploded on impact when it landed.

SAB wasted no time getting back to his truck, they were there too long and in moments that area would be crawling with FBI, Mercenaries and Police. "Here you're going to need this." SAB said as they got into the truck. "Climb in the back and keep them off us, I have to get within range of my help."

"Then let's go" Idris said slamming his door behind him. Idris didn't need to walk around to the back of the truck. With his short legs he climbed over the seats and comfortably sat in a space that would have been impossible for an average size man to sit. He placed a .223 caliber H&K on each side of him then grabbed the bag he was lugging around all night that Kawi packed for him.

Idris called Hassan and Al Amin to see how far they were from their destination. They were less than three minutes out which meant they were only a few minutes behind him. Idris sat his phone down and picked up the Uzi as he watched approaching traffic, a bus, two cars and a minivan. One of the cars and the bus sped by them, the minivan kept a safe distance as a car with two woman approached at a steady speed.

Halfway through the block the minivan picked up speed and the doors on both sides slid open and men from both sides opened fire. "I got um" Idris yelled out to SAB as he returned fire. Out of nowhere a barrage of bullets swept across the Escalade coming from a side street. "Aaahh, I'm hit." Idris hollered dropping his weapon.

The moment the minivan seen Idris was hit they accelerated to full speed and SAB jammed on the brakes. "Hold on" SAB shouted as he turned and let off a round of shots into the fast approaching minivan that was trying to come to a stop and get out of the line of fire at the same time. The driver got hit and the minivan went out of control side swiping the Escalade sending it spinning.

When the Escalade stopped spinning it was facing traffic and there was the car that ambushed them from the side street and shot them up hitting Idris and SAB was out of bullets. He threw his gun out the window then stepped on the gas "BANG" SAB smashed right into the car. He couldn't see who was in it, the car was so small it was practically under the truck.

SAB jammed on the accelerator one more time to get over the hump and the truck flying off the car about to turn over in mid air until, "BANG" an oncoming garbage truck slammed into the Escalade spinning it in a circle while it was still in mid air. The Escalade managed to land on all four wheels and bounced. "Are you still with me back there?" SAB shouted looking for any sign of life from Idris.

"Barely" Idris replied as he struggled to sit up and see where they were. Idris used his last bit of strength to raise his arm, "Turn down this way." He said directing SAB off his path. SAB looked to where he was pointing and turned without any questions.

\*       \*       \*       \*       \*       \*       \*       \*       \*       \*

"We have a visual a Black SUV approaching, it's an Escalade on Tillary coming our way please advice." Agent Marlo sat for a moment and looked at his partner while waiting for command. The command came back loud and clear for everyone to hold their positions and maintain radio silence.

Not even seconds later Agent Marlo's cell phone vibrated. He didn't recognize the number and had reservations about answering.

"We're neutral you got a minute," His partner Kristic encouraged. Marlo answered his cell phone as his partner watched the Escalade sit at the light two blocks off. "Yes" was the first word Agent Marlo spoke then he listened for less than a minute then "Yes" was the last word he spoke.

Kristic seen that wild bug eyed glance Marlo gave him after finishing his call."You remember what we said we would do if we ever got that call?" Agent Marlo asked Kristic in a low secretive tone.

"Yeah whatever it takes....in good reason," Agent Kristic said to make sure they were talking about the same thing.

"Is stopping a terrorist and defector good enough reason?" Marlo asked as he fixed his focus on the black Escalade with the sniper rifle.

Kristic didn't have time to think about it, it wasn't his call Marlo got the call and now Marlo was posted behind the sniper rifle.

Either way 9 agents were killed, 4 Nassau County Police, 2 NYPD and 7 ex-military (Cortex Mercenaries) and the men responsible were on Tillary heading to safety at Cadman Plaza. Marlo's window of opportunity was closing, he wasn't waiting for Kristic's approval but Kristic had to back his play and cover ground level making sure the deed was complete.

# TERRORIST IN BROOKLYN

"Shit" Agent Marlo shouted as the Escalade passed before him. Marlo was set up for distance and the Escalade was right under him. Agent Marlo took his best shot blowing out the back tire causing the truck to swerve and skid to a stop three yards out.

Marlo squeezed off three controlled shots through the top driver side of the truck then he opened fire on the rest of the truck with sporadic shots until he seen Kristic approaching the Escalade with his gun drawn prepared to finish the job.

Kristic couldn't see through the tinted glass in the truck. He circled the truck with hurried steps as his heart raced. Marlo watched anxiously from the roof top unable to see if his shots were affective. He watched as Kristic made it around to the front of the Escalade, Kristic dropped his gun and fell to his knees as he shouted calling on God.

Marlo couldn't make out what Kristic shouted, he let off a quick round of shots into the truck "Pop" "Pop" "Pop" Kristic jumped to his feet. "No, no, nooo." He said as he tried to move forward but dropped to his knees again holding his head. "No." he said one last time.

By the time Agent Marlo made it off the roof, the streets were filled with FBI, NYPD and emergency units. Everyone stood around the Black Escalade. When Agent Marlo approached the crowd parted allowing him exclusive front row viewing of his work.

## CHAPTER TWENTY

**Agent Brinsky sat back idly staring at her phone** trying to make sense of her call from Special Agent Black inquiring into the death of Supreme Court Judge, *'What's this case got to do with that?'* Brinsky questioned herself as she curled her top lip and arched her right eye leaving an expression that showed the perplexity of the question she pondered.

Freedom of expression, something spoke of in the U.S. Constitution but rarely practiced in the 21$^{st}$ century. It wasn't like no one was allowed to express themselves, people just choose not to as they go to and from with their poker faces. With the constant glares of suspicion that eventually is exhausted by the reality of being over worked, living to pay bills while you awaited life's next dilemma, not Agent Brinsky.

By the expressive gaze she held and her tenacity for challenging that which had no bearing on how her day would start or end, it was obvious Caitlyn Elizabeth Brinsky was beyond that cycle of worries and fears, at least for herself. It had everything to do with her new job or Special Agent Black which was one in the same.

Which brought on another question that had her baffled as of late, what was preventing the so eager to express herself Brinsky from doing so when it came to personal matters of Christopher Black.

# TERRORIST IN BROOKLYN

It wasn't until the phone rang did Agent Brinsky realize she was sitting on the edge of her chair, half dressed and oblivious to time or the fact that she left her front door wide open from the time she received her call from SAB. At which time she dropped her takeout Chinese food on the counter and forgot about everything at the sound of his voice, and she has been sitting there since.

She thought it was him calling back but instead it was a more familiar voice. "Surprise!" he said then continued before she could respond. "How's daddy's little girl?"

"Hey dad." Brinsky answered casually. She was surprised but not giving her father the delight of knowing it. "I am alright, just getting in." She replied looking around her apartment acknowledging it for the first time.

"I'm in town for a minute and I thought we could catch a bite before I head back home."

"I just picked Chinese food but-"

"Your mother and I just had Chinese last night. My treat, see you in a few," He insisted before she could get in another word and hung up.

*'What was he doing in New York?'* Brinsky asked herself knowing that her mother told her last night that her father was staying in Washington for a new position he was suddenly offered. Brinsky thought suspiciously of it as she retraced her steps back to the door putting on the clothes she took off as she entered the apartment ten minutes ago.

"Yes something's wrong." She said audibly as she stopped in her tracks looking at the Chinese food on the counter where she left it. Her father and mother didn't have Chinese food last night because he was in Washington and her mother ate salad with wine as they spoke on the phone last night.

\*      \*      \*      \*      \*      \*      \*      \*      \*      \*

Mr. Brinsky tackled his daughter with a big hug as she stepped out her building. "You should have told me you were down here dad, I could have come straight down or you could have come up." Brinsky said firmly then gave her father a kiss on the cheek.

"If I surprised you maybe I caught your admirers off guard as well."

Agent Brinsky was about to turn and look around for these admirers her father was referring to, but then she caught herself and the sudden smirk on her face told her father she understood. Mr. Brinsky just smiled then led his daughter to his car.

"What are you doing in New York I thought you were suppose to be in Washington to see about a new Job with the new administration?"

"I was," he replied grimly. "I drove all the way there to hear about the new agenda."

Brinsky offered a faint smile. *'I hope he isn't going to proposition me again.'* She thought to herself thinking about the last time he visited her about getting her an administrative job with him. "You can go a lot further making the laws then trying to enforce them" he told her trying to convince her as he has for the last year since she joined the Bureau.

Being his only child was not easy especially since everyone involved would have been happier if she was a "HE" when she was born. Nevertheless little Caitlyn weathered the storm and learned sports, even got pass her Tom Boy faze. She thought he would be proud when she came home on his birthday to surprise him telling him she was a G-Man. "Not my little girl!" He shouted. That bordered on hypocritical for him and confusion for her and may explain why since then she now questioned everything, taking nothing else for granted.

At 24 she was used to wearing pants. The idea of carrying a gun and people shuddering when she said FBI in her firmest voice was also appealing to her. Add the intrigue and her natural quest for query she found her home. She dyed her blonde hair black and moved to the one place she knew daddy couldn't impose, New York.

Mr. Brinsky opened the passenger side door for his daughter then took a casual look around for anything or anyone that looked suspicious as he made his way to the driver side. "CONFIDENTAL" the folder that sat in the passenger seat read. Brinsky scooped it up as she flopped in the seat and shut the door behind her.

"Oooooo confidential!" Brinsky teased as she waved the folder at her father. "The big Washington man and all his top secrets," She added.

Mr. Brinsky smirked. He and his daughter always had an honest, open ended relationship which made it easier for the both of them to tell the other what they were thinking. Which turned out

ANTHONY BREWER

to be that more convenient for them both since she left home, which meant the little time they did see each other wasn't used up with small talk.

"I heard they've been keeping an eye on you." Mr. Brinsky began as he started his car and wasted no time in pulling off and checking his rear view mirror to see if anyone pulled off behind them. "How about an ear, have you checked for that?"

Brinsky looked at her father not understanding what he was saying at first until he returned glances giving her a peculiar look. "Oh eyes and ears, real cute dad." Brinsky conceded with a smile as she leaned over nudging her father with her elbow. "What's that, CIA code words or something."

"Take a look at the folder." He demanded firmly. Caitlyn startled by her father's tone glared at him as she opened the confidential folder that rested on her lap. Her heart skipped a beat and her chest was suddenly tight. It took her a few seconds to recognize the photo, it looked like a photo of her during training in Quantico.

Her mind got stuck in gear for a moment as she stared at the stamp over her photo in red ink big block letters that read COMPROMISED. After studying the photo further she realized it was not a Quantico photo. As she turned the pages her suspicions were confirmed the photo along with the information predated her induction into the FBI by at least two years.

"The FBI and the CIA are not the only information agencies." He stated emphatically.

"I know father that there are private agencies that dig deeper than the Bureau, but what's this compromised business about?"

~ 204 ~

Agent Brinsky turned and gave her father a piercing look. "Why exactly did you come and see me?"

The car held a dead silence as Agent Brinsky awaited a reply and Mr. Brinsky made an unexpected u-turn and parked as he watched the oncoming traffic that would have been behind him. Something he read in an espionage book, a trick that would put him face to face with anyone following him.

"I've been on pins and needles since I left Washington." He admitted satisfied he was not being followed. He looked at his daughter and told his story of how he made it to Washington first before he told her the story she wanted to hear about why he came to New York.

The President elect was putting his cabinet together and a lot of names were being thrown around, Mr. Brinsky's name being one of them that was contacted. Mr. Brinsky never put his name in the hat so it was a pleasant surprise. The initial phase of the interview was mainly security related concerns so an array of questions was presented to Mr. Brinsky.

"The questions all seemed standard, I know firsthand considering me and the President of the United States of America will be on a first name bases at some point, they had a job to do." He paused "But I got concerned when they started asking more question about you than me. Does the name Senator Clarkson ring any bells?"

Agent Brinsky thought about it for a moment then shook her head the name didn't ring a bell. "What state?" Brinsky asked.

## ANTHONY BREWER

"He's a good old Texas boy and good friend to former President Borish. I remember his name because we had to pass something through the Ways and Means Committee and he was chairing it."

Mr. Brinsky paused again this time he looked as his daughter, "Actually the interview was going good until they mentioned Caitlyn Elizabeth Brinsky and her involvement with known terrorist. Their exact words were; withholding vital information in an ongoing domestic terrorist investigation conducted by the Bureau that could have international repercussions," Mr. Brinsky stated as a matter factly as possible. He went on for a couple of more minutes about how his job he did not get yet, depended on his daughter's cooperation.

After he finished he let out a roaring yarn. "Now you want to tell me what's going on?" he asked politely.

That was a good question, one she couldn't answer at the moment. Her father watched as she shook her head back and forth. "What do you mean you're not going to tell me or-'

"Dad!" Agent Brinsky raised her index finger. "I need a minute. You surprise me talking about dinner and ambush me with this. I need a minute, I got a lot going on right now."

"I already know about the rogue FBI agent, what I need to know is how deep you're in it with him?"

"I'm with him if that's what you want to know, probably the only one." Brinsky replied without a second hesitation or regret.

"As I figured." Mr. Brinsky replied confirming his suspicions why they called him in the first place. He had been following the reports on Sandi since they began and so has special interest groups invested in its outcome.

Then Special Agent Blacks name popped up and so did Mr. Brinsky's radar since he knew his daughter worked with him and he expected there would be some backlash to fall his daughter's way.

Senator Clarkson knew all this before he called on Mr. Brinsky which will explain the only reason he called Mr. Brinsky in the first place. Mr. Brinsky would have respected Clarkson more if he would have said squeeze your daughter for us and we'll return the favor.

Mr. Brinsky was a politician also so he knew how the game worked, but since the Senator went about it that way made Mr. Brinsky ask a few question of his own.

Not really knowing what was going on he asked all the wrong questions of course, but ask enough stupid questions and soon someone will ask you a question like; "Why are you so concerned with a has been, Clarkson's on the way out with his crew?" Peter Stoller an old friend that worked in Justice Department with Mr. Brinsky many moons ago asked.

"In fact." Stoller continued. "He is not on his way out, he's out. It was a big thing when the new President came in, every network was there and watched President Borish and his flunkies clear out of the White House or should I say Black House as one reported noted."

"It sounds worse in Spanish Casa de Negro, I like Casa Blanca better." Mr. Brinsky admitted. Stoller was still at the Justice

ANTHONY BREWER

Department and since Mr. Brinsky wasn't quite sure which way the wind was blowing just yet, he didn't say anything more to Stoller about his suspicions. That was a couple hours ago when Mr. Brinsky jumped on I-95 straight for New York to find out what his daughter got herself into.

"Daddy" Brinsky said as she slid her hand into her bag. "You did come alone, right?"

Mr. Brinsky looked up at the six men approaching his car carrying fully automatic weapons. "Who in the hell-?" he asked as one of the men opened the driver side door and yanked Mr. Brinsky out of the car placing a gun to his head, while the other men aimed their guns at agent Brinsky.

"Get out of the car and leave your gun on the seat." The man who held the gun to Mr. Brinsky's head demanded.

Agent Brinsky slowly removed her hand from her bag revealing her gun. At the sight of it, the men gripped their weapons tightly. Brinsky laid the gun beside her then clinched her bag as she stepped out of the car.

"What do you want?" she asked the man who held her father.

"It's not what I want that you should concern yourself with." The man replied as two men grabbed Agent Brinsky by her arm and led her off to a waiting car. Before they reached the car the passenger side door opened and a man stepped out.

Agent Brinsky strained her eyes to see through the darkness and the bad lighting on the side of the road didn't help. She was unable to see his face but something about his features stood out.

A chill ran through her body as the man stepped into view and managed a smile on his cold stone carved face. "No introductions are needed Agent Brinsky, but you do look surprised. How long did you and your coworker think you'll could run around disturbing progress before the two of you were held accountable?" Dercole asked then gestured with a nod of the head to the man who was holding a gun to Mr. Brinsky's head. "This only works if you're watching."

Agent Brinsky turned to look at her father, in the second it took her to blink her eyes the man holding her father pulled the trigger shooting Mr. Brinsky in the head. She heard the shot and seen her father fall to the ground. She didn't actually see him shoot her father so she didn't think he was dead. She took a step away from the man holding her as if she was running to her father then quickly stepped backwards forcefully striking him in his solar plexus.

The man dropped instantly as Agent Brinsky ran to her father ignoring the other armed men. "Dad get up, Daddy!" she screamed. It was her blood stained hands that clutched her father's head that told her he was dead. She lifted her blood stained hands before her face and looked at them as if she never seen blood before. Her eyes dropped down to her lifeless father then rose slowly and stopped on Dercole.

"Now that I have your attention." He growled taking a step closer so she could hear every word. "You know too much and your father was a fast learner. Your mother on the other hand does not have a clue, so she could actually get out of this without a scratch. But that is completely up to you." He instructed then asked her the one question he needed the answer to, "Besides you and Agent Black who else knows about Project Skeleton?"

Agent Brinsky sat there nonresponsive just staring at Dercole. Dercole kneeled down clinched a hand full of her hair and shook her to wake her from out of her stupor or shock whatever it was, but he wanted an answer.

"So that you know-" Mr. Dercole added. "Special Agent Black was killed moments ago. I tell you this so you don't think someone is riding in here guns blazing to rescue you. Now tell me who else knows about Project Skeleton?" He asked one final time. From the way she looked at him he realized she was not in shock and understood every word.

"Fine have it your way!" Dercole nodded to the man standing over her with the gun to her head and turned his back.

"Wait" Mr. Dercole said the moment his cell phone rang.

Mr. Dercole stood there quietly listening into the phone as Carlton Richard shouted at the top of his lungs. Mr. Dercole could not make out exactly what he was saying through all the yelling, but one thing he said that was clear. Special Agent Black was not dead and if so Mr. Richard had every reason to be upset.

Special Agent Black being dead or alive bared no consequences to Mr. Richard's rage he could have Black killed at anytime. What infuriated Mr. Richard, he was trying to clean up an old mess and someone just shot the New York Police Commissioner making a new one.

Mr. Richard never monitored the outcome of the rough stuff, but he was keeping his eye on the one distraction that could alter his overall objective. After he finished venting his frustrations he changed his tone and spoke clearly so Mr. Dercole could understand every word.

"Forget about our friends in the Bureau they have their own problems, they just shot the NYPD Police Commissioner. Pay the Deputy Director another visit, this time thank him for his services!"

"What about our problem?" Mr. Dercole asked. There was silence on the other end of the phone.

Mr. Richard was hinging on leaving Sandi the Terrorist and Agent Black the Traitor for the American justice system. Particularly with Sandi and Black's name surrounding the shooting of the Commissioner they would get the rap for that and maybe the dead FBI Deputy Director they would find in the morning.

"Say goodnight to the deputy and come back home. All the damage points back to Sandi and Agent Black so our work is done. Everyone else is dead and no one will believe two Muslim terrorist."

"I have Agent Black's partner here."

"Wipe your hands of that and move on to your next job." Mr. Richard firmly instructed then did something he rarely ever done, second guessed himself. "No, bag her and put her someplace safe she could come in handy in the event our special agent gets resourceful and evades the lynch mob."

## CHAPTER TWENY ONE

**The moment Special Agent Black turned** off Tillary Avenue his cell phone rang. The name on the display read Brinsky. "Where are you?" he asked before he could get the phone to his ear. When he didn't get an answer he was about to repeat his question but was distracted by the high beam of a SUV that pulled up behind him.

"What's our status back there?" SAB asked Idris.

SAB placed his cell phone on the seat next to him and torqued his body around to get a better look at the nonresponsive Idris and the truck that pulled up behind him. The truck flashed their high beams three times and stopped. SAB slowed down and gradually came to a stop some distance from the truck behind him then went to check on Idris.

As soon as he climbed out of the Escalade the passenger side door to the white Tahoe truck behind him opened and a tall man about 6'5" stepped out and casually walked towards SAB. His casual demeanor put SAB at ease enough where he didn't see any harm in walking to the back of his truck where Idris was. Worst case scenario he could grab one of Idris's guns.

When SAB open the back door compartment Idris just sat there staring at him. He barely moved and his breathing was laborious but he had a relaxed almost sublime look. Still SAB knew something was wrong. In the darkness SAB was not able to see the blood coming from Idris's neck and upper torso from where the bullets got through his vest.

SAB reached into the truck and picked up the gun that laid besides Idris as the tall man approached the Escalade. That moment SAB bent over to pick up the gun he seen the pool of blood. Idris seen the startled look on Sajud's face and managed a smile.

SAB didn't realize he was holding his breath until the second he exhaled and looked away from Idris to look at the tall man who was coming up behind him.

"I'm Hussein." The tall man said introducing himself so SAB could stop pointing the gun he held tightly against his hip ready to fire.

"How did you know it was us in the truck?" SAB asked as he pushed pass Hussein to retrieve his phone and call for an ambulance.

"I was the one who told Idris you'll needed a black Escalade and where to meet me at."

"Damn!" SAB said when he realized he left Agent Brinsky on the phone. "Hello" he shouted into the phone and still he got no reply. He pressed his ear to the phone and listened harder when he heard someone talking on the other end. SAB jumped, startled from the sound of a gunshot that came through the phone.

"Do I have your attention now?" A voice asked on the other end of the phone. The voice sounded familiar and it only took a second for Mr. Dercole's name to register.

"You know too much and your father is a fast learner." Mr. Dercole added.

'Her father?' SAB thought. 'How did her father get into the picture?' SAB asked himself then looked at Hussein who was pulling his dead cousins body out of the truck. SAB shook his head, all of this was getting way out of hand. He put his Bluetooth in his ear to listen for any useful information that could locate Agent Brinsky while he went to help Hussein carry Idris's body to his truck.

Hussein brushed SAB aside he needed no help. He cupped Idris's body in his arms and delicately carried him and laid him in the back seat of his truck then handed SAB Idris's phone. "You're going to need this. He wants you to finish this and he said to take his message with you, those were his last words."

SAB stood there speechless as he watched Hussein climb into his truck. "But I will need Sandi," SAB finally said.

Hussein started his truck and pulled up in front of SAB. "Who wants Sandi the Federal Agent or Sajud the Muslim?"

"They are one in the same." SAB replied.

"Easier said than done, but of course you know that. If you have to choose which one to be, like choosing a side or something, choose to me a man correcting a wrong, which wrong is up to you. Sandi is on his way to the airport. They didn't think you would make it this far so I don't think they will be waiting, I suggest you hurry."

"Are you the one who killed the men in front of Sandi's house?" SAB asked.

TERRORIST IN BROOKLYN

"Why do you have a problem with that?" Hussein asked firmly.

"No. You said I was in a hurry, I was hoping you killed a few more of them for me they have my partner."

Hussein had two problems with that, Idris was the only reason he got involved in any of this business in the first place. Hussein motioned to the back seat where his cousin laid then looked at SAB.

"You ever hear the expression know when to cut your losses? This is the reason why I am not on that plane going to Iraq, my part in all this ended with my obligation to family. My obligation to you my brother ended when I gave you Idris's phone that will get you where you need to be to handle your business with likeminded people. As for your partner needing help you need to dial 911," Hussein said then saluted SAB as he put his truck in gear.

"Your obligations don't end with your cousin. Your obligations end when you have fulfilled them all." SAB shouted. "As a Muslim and citizen of this country you have an obligation to enjoin what is right and forbid what is wrong. You said Idris wanted me to finish this, I need your help." SAB pulled his cell phone out his pocket and handed it to Hussein. "They keep saying the Muslim is the terrorist, let's pull the curtain back and expose the real terrorist in Brooklyn.

Hussein wasn't moved by the speech, reluctantly he reached out and took the phone. "All you have to do is catch a plane me on the other hand?" That was SAB's cue to fill Hussein in on what he needed to know. From what Idris told SAB about Hussein's

~ 215 ~

training and the work he already seen Hussein put in SAB wouldn't have to do more than tell him how to get Mr. Dercole's attention.

*"Pull back the curtain and show who the real terrorist is."* Hussein thought out loud of SAB's last words as he watched SAB pull off in a rush to catch a plane. 'What the hell is a terrorist in the first place?' Hussein asked himself considering only last week he assisted in blowing up a building and participating in a massacre of a police station full of police.

"What would that make me?" he asked himself as he looked at himself in the rear view mirror as if the answer to that would be stamped on his forehead. Instead he saw the body of his lifeless cousin lying on the back seat. "A fool!" he answered as he slammed his fist against the staring wheel in anger. He was against this from the very beginning for only one reason, he knew this kind of thing never ended well.

But deep down inside he knew everything that happened was predestined. They didn't go looking for Sandi he was literally dropped in their laps. Second guessing if they should have helped him or killed him after he witnessed Idris kill a federal informant wouldn't help now. The only thing Hussein took out of all this was in each scenario they had to make a decision and they did, the right decision.

What made it feel predestined or fate is how things happened. Kawi's brother David would have been shot regardless what they did or did not do. Sandi's arrival only allowed them to handle Kawi's situation as forcefully and efficient as they did almost like they administered a punishment that came from a higher power.

So Sandi was help in something they didn't even see coming that was predestined to happen, and they helped Sandi in similar affair needing correcting.

Hussein couldn't go anywhere with a dead body in the back of his truck so his first stop was the Mosque. Imam Ibraheem was not surprised and did not grieve, he felt the burden of not knowing what was going to happen to his son lifted.

Without a word he took Idris's body and began to prepare for his Janazah prayer, there was no need delaying it and there was always the chance Federal or other authorities could come looking for his son. He didn't have a problem giving him to them living, there would be no problem in his death.

He washed and wrapped Idris in ceremonial white cloth and wasted no time performing the Janazah prayer with those who were able to come on such short notice. When he was finished he turned and looked at Hussein for the first time asking for an explanation.

"You are his elder cousin who he followed all his life. Tell me why my son died and what you didn't do to stop this." The Imam softly asked. It was a two part rhetorical question that had the same answer, he didn't stop him from getting into whatever that brought his death. Hussein turned his face away from the Imam unable to look into his heavy eyes.

"Is this over, do I have to expect anyone else walking through that door?" Imam Ibraheem asked looking at the same door Hussein glared at. That was another question Hussein could not answer, he couldn't control who came through that door.

Hussein made eye contact with the Imam for the first time, "Not if I can help it."

"And what happened to the Muslim agent?"

"He is on his way to Iraq with Kawi, Al Amin and Sandi where he and Sandi believe the root of this problem is."

The Imam did not know how to reply to that because he didn't know what was going on aside from his belief that they involved themselves in something that was not their business.

That was the Imam's emotions getting the best of him because he already concluded when he first spoke to Idris at Hussein's house about all this. He and Idris both agreed it was God who chose what you went through, Sandi, Idris, Al Amin, Kawi, Hasssan and even SAB only had the choice of how you went through it.

He conveyed that to Hussein and instantly Hussein felt his guilt lifted, but more importantly in so many words the Imam said the same thing Hussein was feeling, this was Qadar, predestined.

Hussein sat in his truck now realizing his fate. He knew what he had to do and it wasn't run or look the other way. He was placed in a position to act and given a direction. The vibration of SAB's cell phone broke Hussein out of his trance. He snatched it off the dash board and looked at the number it read Brinsky on the display.

If Cortex had Brinsky like SAB said it was Cortex calling. Hussein studied the phone for a moment thinking what to do. "Yeah!" Hussein answered as if it was his own phone then listened, it was a man's voice.

## TERRORIST IN BROOKLYN

"You can have your partner back just give us Sandi and we can be friends again. Everyone still thinks we're on the same team," Mr. Dercole instructed.

"How about you make a good faith effort and I will tell you where Sandi is and how you can get him."

"Faith is what your people thrive off, it doesn't do much for me Mr. Sajud. Give me your Muslim brother and I'll give you your woman, fair trade no robbery," Mr. Dercole assured.

Hussein didn't know what to say, what would Special Agent Black say. "What makes you think I have him?" Hussein asked.

"I thought you were not one for wasting time or a life!" Mr. Dercole insisted as he stood by Agent Brinsky who was tied to a chair and gagged. "We will get him rather you give him to us or not. This way saves time and bloodshed for the both of us," Mr. Dercole added.

"I'll save us both some time and come to you and we can pick up Sandi together with one condition you let my partner go now or there is no negotiation. You refuse I will get find you and kill you just like I did O' Patrick and Doyle." Hussein paused for a moment, "And remember this is your only option. The Police Commissioner was shot only hours ago and Brooklyn is on lockdown."

"Which means your hands are tied also, let's stop with the charades."

"I don't need to leave the Brooklyn to get Sandi a Special Opt Team has been assembled to bring Sandi in." Hussein informed Mr. Dercole and got no response.

Special Opt registered with Mr. Dercole and different acronyms ran through his head, SOF, CSAR, USASOC, or even SOG, all highly elite special force teams that operate on foreign soil handling delicate assignments.

"Sandi is not even in America." Mr. Dercole concluded.

"That is correct, hence my suggestion you let the girl go and we wait together until my team brings in Sandi."

Now that Mr. Dercole realized Sandi was back in Iraq he didn't need Agent Black's help in retrieving him, the negotiations were over.

Mr. Dercole was tempted to kill Agent Brinsky were she sat but his last orders were to keep her alive, but Agent Black on the other hand. "Deal" Mr. Dercole said enthusiastically. "The ball is in your court I'll let your partner go, but to keep you honest I will release her when you arrive I'm sending a car for you."

"No thanks, I'll come to you then you can release her."

"Deal" Mr. Dercole replied, hung up and wasted no time calling Mr. Richard to inform him that Sandi was right there in Iraq under his nose.

\*      \*      \*      \*      \*      \*      \*      \*      \*      \*

*'Was that the hard part or the easy part?'* Hussein questioned himself as he now had to figure out how he was going to pull this off. He was by himself meeting people he didn't know and even worse, ran the chance of getting Agent Brinsky killed if he made one wrong move.

Hussein was parked in his truck sitting behind the Mosque's secondary exit. He was alarmed when he seen someone came out that exit because it was not used by many with the exception of those exiting the Mosque from the secret door in the boiler room.

Instantly he recognized Mujaheed as he turned towards Hussein's truck as if he knew exactly where Hussein was. Mujaheed glanced at his watch and crossed to meet Hussein in hurried steps. "I am surprised you are still sitting here, figuring out your next move?" Mujaheed asked.

Hussein looked at Mujaheed without replying and Mujaheed returned the look. "Are we going to sit here all night or are you going to finish what you started?"

Hussein had a baffled look on his face, that spelled how much do you know, or more importantly how did he know. The answer became obvious after a moment of consideration seeing him come out of the Mosque where Imam Ibraheem more than likely told him everything.

Mujaheed shook his head. "No the Imam didn't tell me anything, he didn't have to. I have been watching you'll since Idris and Hassan dropped that body in the park," Mujaheed informed Hussein.

He went on to tell him he watched everything else thereafter from the shoot out at Sandi's house to the last incident that got Idris killed. "I can tell you more, probably more than you know but we have to move." Mujaheed said.

Hussein looked at Mujaheed then took the truck out of park as he eased it into the street. Mujaheed was Hussein's cousin, not like Idris who was his first cousin from his father's side. Mujaheed was more like a distant cousin who came along when they went to the Madrasa in Long Island that was equivalent a Muslim Junior High School and they were all around fourteen years old.

He was the only distant cousin out of all of them so that was his excuse to keep his distance. He enlisted in the service his first chance and that kept the distance until Borish Jr. came into office and it was open season on Muslims in Iraq and around the world. Mujaheed opted out as a Consciences Objector, he didn't sign up for that.

"I have somewhere to be in less than an hour." Hussein instructed.

"I am sure the Imam wanted you to finish this. I am only curious how you intended on doing that?"

Hussein held Sajud's phone up in the air then told Mujaheed about his conversation with Dercole. "I was sitting her trying to figure out how I can do this without getting the Agent killed or myself for that matter. Do you have any suggestions?" Hussein asked.

"First of all, they're not in Redhook." Mujaheed assured as he began with directions to where they was holding Brinsky. Hussein was surprised but not entirely. He was about to ask how did he know but Mujaheed did say he was following them.

They were not Redhook they were at the Navy Yard and Mujaheed already had an idea how to get in. After Hussein heard his plan he only had two words, "Absolutely not!" Hussein shouted.

"Then what do you suggest, you just told me you were sitting there clueless when I jumped into the car."

"911"

"These are Mercenaries you forget, you took out a few yourself. They will eat the boys in blue as a snack. Something like what you'll did to the 87th!"

"We dial 911 for back up, distraction, help, or whatever you want to call it, but at least when it is said and done, it will be said and done and we wouldn't have chose a side and we're putting this thing to rest. We are saving a Federal Agent and stopping terrorist, hence the 911."

What's the federal equivalent to 911?" Mujaheed asked. Hussein waved the phone in Mujaheed's face for the second time. "Special Agent Black's personal phone, everyone's number is in here." Hussein smiled at the prospect of the upper hand.

## CHAPTER TWENTY TWO

**Mr. Richard sat on the edge of his desk** as he gazed over his 40 billion dollar oil complex. He looked through the window of his main office that was strategically placed in the center of the complex without anything obstructing his view. A clear path of vision over the things important to him, he only wished his vision over his political future was this clear.

His path of entry was clearing up and opposition was little to none. Actually, he was welcomed by men of similar thinking. There was only the small matter of him cleaning up a few things that could spoil the atmosphere once he set things in full motion. Years of hard work, billions of dollars in investments and uncompromising international affiliations could easily be destroyed with one skeleton from the pass emerging at the wrong time in the future.

Hence Project Skeleton was finally going to end in less than one hour. Mr. Richard glanced at his watch then strolled over to the window that gave him a clear view over the main entrance of the complex. The moment he got the call from Mr. Dercole telling him Sandi was in Iraq, Mr. Richard told him to finish up and hurry back.

Mr. Richard was beyond himself with excited about the good news he told Mr. Dercole not only to kill both Agents Brinsky and Black he said, "You were right about getting rid of the Deputy

Director which means the Deputy was wrong about not wiping out all the Blacks." Those words were music to Mr. Dercole's ears.

After Mr. Richard dispatched those orders he called Derrick Francis of Sheppard and shared with him the good news. Finding a special opt team in Iraq was not an easy task for even Francis who controlled over 40,000 Sheppard employees and had influence over a majority of the mercenaries and War Lords in his region.

The only obstacle Mr. Francis faced was special opt teams didn't registered with the United Nations and always came and gone under the radar, they moved in secret.

As a backup Mr. Richard offered a five million dollar reward to whatever group brought in Sandi. With hopes the Special Opt Team that found him would cash Sandi in, for what came up to a half of million a man since a team would average eight to ten men for a small discreet task such as theirs.

Within the hour Mr. Richard got a phone call saying Sandi was located. Mr. Richard sent out retrieval escorts and was now waiting for Sandi's arrival. '*Things that are meant to be just turn out to be that easy.*' Mr. Richard reasoned as watched a convoy of military trucks enter through the main entrance of his complex, lead by his escorts.

Mr. Richards took the brief case from under his desk and carried it down to the lower level and waited for his prize. The men entered in three groups, Mr. Richard's escort's escorted the four captured men and the Special Opt Team there to collect their reward.

The four captures were Sandi, and three other men of Arab decent. Mr. Richard welcomed the Special Opt Team and thanked them for their cooperation. He studied the men before considering offering them part time employment, for any future situations they could assist each other in this manner.

There was something familiar about one of the members of the Special opt Team that brought a feeling that has been haunting him. *'Finally after so many years and he looks just like his mother, Mariam Sajud.'* Mr. Richards thought to himself as he studied SAB from the corner of his eye.

She was probably the only ghost he knew. Her death was the only one that haunted him. An American woman who was literally in the wrong place, at the wrong time, working for a man who reached his expiration.

But one thing for sure her son will not be a ghost to him because he gave Christopher Black too many opportunities to get out the way, opportunities that he did not give his mother Mariam. After her everyone else on her blood line would be just a casualty to one sin that would bring the same ghost to him, hers.

Dercole wasn't there, so Mr. Richard had to handle this exchange himself and whatever plot that was cooked up to bring Special Agent Black to his door step.

"Secure them in the lower level." Mr. Richard commanded then called Mr. Francis to alert him of the situation. This was the last straw and every caution was going to be taken. Mr. Richard then called on Dercole.

## TERRORIST IN BROOKLYN

Dercole was delighted by the news that Sandi was captured with his conspirators. Dercole even took credit for it. There was only one problem, if Special Agent Black was going to be captured in Iraq who was he talking to less than an hour ago on Black's phone.

This didn't change anything for Dercole he was still going to proceed to meet the voice on the other end of the phone and finish this once and for all. Dercole wanted to clean house which included the last remaining living relative, Mr. Black Sr.

Dercole sent his men to the agreed upon meeting location and peered from afar for his visitors. The location was a warehouse in a desolate section of Redhook in Brooklyn. Dercole left a constellation prize for his visitors, ten pounds of plastic explosives.

Dercole sat patiently waiting for the cavalry to show, he had no way of finding out who was acting as Agent Black. Though he was curious, it would not matter once they breached the warehouse. Black's stand in would get what was intended for Black.

A full hour passed and no one showed. Dercole was concerned, then his phone rang it was one of his men. "We were hit, we were hit," he repeated almost in disbelief. Dercole didn't ask any questions. He discontinued the call and continued on to his next task. He was on a schedule was behind schedule and should have never taken the time to play that game once he discover Agent Black was not part of the equation. Dercole intended to vent his frustration elsewhere.

\*     \*     \*     \*     \*     \*     \*     \*     \*     \*

It was not the FBI's Deputy Directors Ramen's opposition to knocking off one of their own that kept Special Agent Black alive, it was Mr. Richard's ambivalence as a result of his guilt of killing SAB's mother that kept Black Jr. and Sr. alive this long.

Dercole only had to decide if he was going to handle Mr. Black Sr. himself or send someone else. 'Why not meet the whole family?' Dercole reasoned as he waited in the kitchen of Mr. Ramen Deputy Director of the Federal Bureau of Investigation. He was already making house calls why not make one more. He could do it before catching his pre dawn flight back to Iraq to join Mr. Carlton Richard.

The Deputy Director took all the necessary precautions any man walking into his home would make. He tapped on the outdoor wall lamp that was flickering, he just placed new bulbs in both lamps.

*'One tap was all it took, but since I am going to be home tomorrow I have an excuse to pull out the good old tool box.'* He thought as he went into his house.

That was his last thought. Dercole came out from behind the darkness of the curtain's shadow before Ramen could turn on the light. Dercole pulled the trigger of his Browning HP twice, he caught Ramen's limp body as he fell and laid him on the floor.

## CHAPTER TWENTY THREE

**Mr. Richard requested the soldiers escort Sandi** to the lower level. When he seen them stall he knew this was part of their plan. The moment he asked himself what were they waiting for, he noticed large numbers of Arabs gaining access to his building and at the same time he heard explosive charges going off throughout his complex. Spontaneously a gun fight ensued between Carlton Richard's escorts and Khalil's men.

Khalil's men were fighting under the banner of liberation, Sandi and Sajud, sought revenge and Al Amin was there in support of Kawi who like Sandi and Sajud thought Carlton Richards was a problem.

"Finally" Sandi grimaced as he approached Mr. Richard who raised his hands in the air as if he was making a surrendering gesture in his defeat.

Special Agent Black's breathing became labored along with everyone else's. His eyes watered, but that did not stop him from seeing side wall panels open and men rush out wearing gas oxygen mask and firing on them. At that moment he realized Richard Carlton was not surrendering he was giving a signal.

Richard Carlton snatched the mask out of the air that was thrown to him and pushed his way through the choking men. That split second meant everything as Kawi, Sajud, Al Amin and the other men with them had to choose between putting on the M95 gas mask that came with their uniform or getting out of the line of fire of Carlton Richard's and Francis men. Going after Carlton Richard was a last thought.

Sandi had no mask or a weapon, he had nothing to stop Carlton Richards from fleeing. Which was more painful, the toxic smoke that was literally choking him to death or the fact that he was so close but yet so far from revenging his family.

That was a question he would never answer, Sandi dropped to the floor unable to hold his breath any longer and collapsed, he died instantly from asphyxia.

Surrounded by several of his men and Sheppard soldiers Richard Carlton made it safely to his office on the upper level. From there he could see everything, his compound was under attack and the men he had trapped that pretended to be Special Opts fought hard. After seven minutes of gunfire the toxic gas cleared several bodies laid there dead.

Outside the main building it seemed like hundreds of Arabs were spread throughout the complex attacking trying to gain control over one building or another for a stronghold but it was not as simple as they thought. Getting onto the Complex was not the hardest part to the contrary, getting out of it was.

Once they made it on to the complex that was sitting in the middle of the desert, they either had to occupy or flee and Richard Carlton was prepared for both scenarios. He would not let them do either, they were trapped. That was the sole purpose behind his location across from Sheppard's headquarters.

In less than an half an hour of gun battle between Khalil's men, Kawi's helpers and other Arabs who signed up for battle against their common foe Cortex was surrounded by U.S. military soldiers ready to subdue any opposition.

Mr. Francis entered Richard Carlton office and stood by him as they shared the moment peering out the window as their forces wiped out all opposition.

"I could almost think you had this planned." Francis said breaking the silence between the two of them.

"But?" Richards asked.

"There was a vital moment in all this you didn't have control. Or you can tell me you seen this coming and was prepared."

Richard Carlton pointed out his window to Francis's private military force and the U.S. military forces crushing the invading forces, "With that kind of power can I ever lose control."

"The real question, will this be enough power to usher you into the Presidency after only couple years as Senator?"

"Political and military power are not the same but to answer your question, I'll settle for Senator in two years, Vice President in four and Commander and Chief in eight."

## CHAPTER TWENTY FOUR

**Dercole had an early 6:15 flight** which meant he could give Mr. Black a wakeup call at 5:15 and make his flight an hour later. The Recreational Center Mr. Black resided in served Dercole well. He found easy access through an alley window through the female's bathroom.

He quietly followed a string of night lights that directed him to the front to the building, then the rear where the interior décor changed only slightly but enough to suit someone's comfort. Dercole's heart started racing to meet the intensity of the moment.

At the glimpse of an open door with furnishings Dercole removed his safety and eased through the door seeing the corner of a bed. He inched quietly approaching with a steady hand, his heart calmed with his breathing.

*'Nice and easy!'* he said to himself as he inched closer to his prey, coming in full view of the bed. The bed was fully made and no one was in it. Dercole's heart began to race again and Dercole eyes quickly began to search the room through the darkness.

It was 5:15 on the dot, the alarm clock radio came on. Dercole was not alarmed he gave it glance and continued, he was not yet discovered and he knew he still had the advantage if Mr. Black was there at all.

After making it to the front of the Center and seeing no possible way for Mr. Black to enter, he seen he had no other way to exit aside from the window. He glanced at his watch, it read 5:19 as the alarm clock radio rambled on about an election in Iraq.

Dercole listened pass the radio and into the darkness. He was not going to discredit the scouting report that Mr. Black was seen entering the Center and did not leave. Dercole cautiously made his way through the Center annoyed by the rambling of the radio disc jockey.

"Breaking News!" The Disc Jockey announced. "We will not be able to take the credit to say we were the first to report this but we will say we are glad to report it."

There was a brief silence, a good silence for Dercole who used it to listen closely before he made his move back towards the bathroom window he entered from.

"I couldn't help it, I had to confirm." The Disc Jockey began. "Federal agents just charged a building lead by Muslims, the same Muslims that were on that notorious MOST WANTED list. And-" he paused with excitement. "They rescued a female federal agent who was allegedly abducted by terrorist."

*'Damn'* Dercole mumbled to himself.

"Damn is what I said too." Mr. Black Sr. said as he stepped up behind Dercole. "Sounds like your type of people and the sad thing about it-"

The same moment Mr. Black paused Dercole spun, he didn't know which way to spin Mr. Black Sr. never made contact by putting the gun to him as Dercole hoped for in a worse case scenario.

**ANTHONY BREWER**

Dercole reached out to nothing but air. Two flashes of light filled the room, it was almost like déjà vu of hours earlier with the Deputy Director. The only difference the hunter became the prey. The only thing that came to Dercole's mind was that look on the Deputy Directors face of surprise, now Dercole had that look and also died with it.

## CHAPTER TWENTY FIVE

**Early retirement conversations** usually served McCarthy's purpose when talking sonority. The actual act of retiring was never as real as it was that moment he knew what he needed to do.

That moment occurred when Hussein called McCarthy on Special Agent Black's phone. "I was told to call this number. Agent Black told me when I found the place you'll find the time, and some help we need to rescue Agent Brinksy." Hussein instructed.

McCarthy knew a call would be coming, he didn't know when. What he didn't know that was the call would be coming from a Most Wanted, that was a twist.

"I am retiring regardless how this turns out, so I get a pass regardless. SAB's out there and Brinsky needs assistance, it doesn't matter who the messenger is we have to move. You boys have to decide where your hearts are," McCathy told the team.

"My loyalty is to my team, my heart goes out to justice." Walton spoke up without giving it a second thought.

"I see everything much clearer from the scope of my rifle." Jenkins admitted. "I'm a safe distance from everything and no one really knows I'm watching them. We hear the word Terrorist so much we become insensitive to the word. Until something like 9/11 and terrorist was not just another word the government used to scare the public to pass another bill.

*ANTHONY BREWER*

I seen those men blow the brains out of innocent men who bowed their heads in pray." Jenkins stood, "And now they have someone from our team."

Simms stood and followed Jenkins to the door he didn't have to say a word, he already knew what he wanted to do he just wanted the right time to do it. Now the verdict was in favoring Special Agent Black.

With the assistance of Hussein and Mujaheed who used them like Cortex used them, Hussein killed Cortex's men as he came in contact with them. Jenkins watched Hussein and Mujaheed work from his scope as they went from room to room towards their destination.

Two men who lived in Brooklyn New York all their lives and never had a day of professional training as killers handled themselves like professionals. Jenkins watched as the two men separated and attacked from different sides of the warehouse to meet at a set point where they thought Brinsky would be.

That was the only opportunity Jenkins had to assist from the large crane that sat in the center of the Navy Yard one hundred feet above ground. By the time Hussein reached Cortex men that were holding Brinsky, they laid in ambush waiting.

The only thing that saved Hussein as he came under fire when he enter the 40 x 60 warehouse space was his long black leather bullet proof trench coat. He immediately ran for cover, "Aagghhh" he yelled out as a bullet ripped through his thigh sending Hussein flying.

Hussein couldn't get a visual on Agent Brinsky, he couldn't return fire. Mujaheed on the other hand watched as they took the bait, all eyes and guns were on Hussein allowing him to come behind the his opposition to the far back wall of the warehouse by the windows.

The moment Mujaheed caught sight of Brinsky he went to opened fire. Before he could pull the trigger the two men standing next to Brinsky dropped as did Mujaheed, but only for a second as he realized that was his back up. Jenkins first two shots were to free Agent Brinsky.

McCarthy covered Hussein as Walton and Simms rushed in returning fire on Cortex men who were trapped and immediately realized they were taking fire from every direction, they surrendered.

"Are you alright?" McCarthy asked Agent Brinsky as he untied her. Brinsky stared pass him with a blank look, her blue eye didn't sparkle and the white of her eyes were red.

She rose without saying a word to McCarthy then picked up a 45. Desert Eagle that sat at her foot from the fallen mercenary. She already seen when Dercole left so it made no sense looking for him, she overheard him speak of a flight to Iraq.

She was going to Iraq to get Dercole, he killed her father. What was surprising was McCarthy, Simms, Jenkins and Walton was going with her. Hussein and Mujaheed insisted on coming along to finish this.

Before they exited the Navy Yard they were surrounded by NYPD, FBI, Coast Guard and local news cameras. Brinsky who was the only one who knew what was going on didn't have time for talk she had a flight to catch.

"We have to give them something and we can move around a lot better without you two." McCarthy told Hussein and Mujaheed. I take since you called me you know what's going on. You'll handle this, we will handle things in Iraq.

Hussein discarded his coat and arsenal, straightened out his kufi and jalabir and winked at Mujaheed, "Showtime." he said as he headed out pass Jenkins and Walton. Hussein had something to talk about and he took it straight to the Attorney General who was in New York as a result of the Police Commissioner getting shot.

It didn't matter how Hussein told it, the story was simple he, Mujaheed, along with FBI agents rescued Agent Brinsky from the same terrorist who was setting up Agent Black.

## CHAPTER TWENTY SIX

**Deputy Director Walter Ramen's body was found** shortly after his death and word traveled to the Director quickly. Covering up one wrong with another was bad enough. Because Special Agent Black was Muslim he became expendable, charged to the war on terrorism. They all had to put the death of his mother behind them before it came back on everyone who covered it up last year and getting rid of SAB was the easiest way.

Killing the Deputy Director and the NYPD Police Commissioner changed everything. Now cortex was expendable and whatever emerged from the death of Mariam Sajud Black would also be charged to Cortex.

Before Brinsky, McCarthy, Simms, Walton, and Jenkins could determine their course of action, the Director had a flight ready for them and ground assistance waiting for them in Iraq.

He informed Agent Black's team he would assist indirectly, if he had to pick a side he backed his men. He had to, Cortex was in Brooklyn with mercenaries killing people and he was not letting the Deputy Ramen or the Bureau take the rap.

Regardless how much the Director knew or what he stood to gain from former President Borish it was the present standing President he had to answer to. Present job security versus what, with Cortex under the gun with the Attorney General ready to set an example to keep his job.

## *ANTHONY BREWER*

The Director knew what he had to do. He could say he was oblivious to all this, which would make him and the Attorney General seem incompetent. Not when the new president was cleaning house.

They were willing to Sacrifice Special Agent Black for progress in Iraq now they was going to sacrifice Cortex for job security at home.

## CHAPTER TWENTY SEVEN

**With the death of Sandi and the capture of Agent Black**, Richard Carlton seen a different picture. He closed the door on project Skeleton and opened his door to a political future.

Nothing the Director of the FBI or the Attorney General could do at this point to alter Richard's appointment as the Republican Senator of Texas.

That part was already prearranged as a result of Carlton Richards accomplishments in Iraq. The United State of America had its first fully functional oil complex based in Iraq. It wasn't the Caspian Sea, but one step at a time.

While Agents McCarthy, Brinsky, Simms, Walton, and Jenkins were retrieving Agent Black from U.S. Military Mr. Richard was on his jet back to America to begin his life a politician.

His first month home in Texas he was welcomed with open arms. There were little to no backlash from Dercole's actions against Agents Black or Brinsky, they were busy clearing themselves of any wrong doing before the house of Professional Responsibility, Attorney General and the Director of the FBI.

Richards enjoyed family time with his three daughters Samantha 3, Heather 9 and Julia 17. There was always a sleepover, pajama party, or birthday party and always a house full of girls. That was one thing Richard had to get use to again.

Today was Julia's 18th Birthday, a special event that was a day before his Senatorial confirmation. After the ceremonial singing of

ANTHONY BREWER

Happy Birthday and cutting of the cake Mr. Richard disappeared and found solace in his study.

With two things to celebrate Mr. Richard opened a bottle of reserved Viellille Brandy and poured it with pride as he thought about its purchase five years ago. He promised himself back then he would not open it until he reached his political platform.

There was a knock on the door. Mr. Richard opened the door to find what looked like one of Heathers 16 year old friends. "Are you looking for Heather?" Mr. Richard asked.

"No I am Julia's friend," The little girl replied as she stepped into the study and looked around with her big wide eyes and bright smile.

"Julia is still down stairs young lady. Would you like me to take you where she's at?"

"No thank you. She told me to ask you for something special for her birthday."

Mr. Richard smiled, *What is my daughter up to now?'* he thought closing the door slightly leaving it cracked. "Okay!" he agreed as he put down his drink and turned to give the young lady his attention.

When he turned to her she leaped onto his chest, her weight knocked him backwards into his recliner, her legs instantly locker around his waist. As he went to push himself up he felt a six inch razor sharp blade on his neck supported by the bulk of the girl's weight. With her little bony legs wrapped around his waist for support he could not move her without the blade cutting his throat.

The knife was so close to his jugular vein he could barely speak much less call for help. "What are you doing?" he asked slowly and cautiously still to be punished by the sharpness of the blade.

"What am I doing?" Tinsia asked herself. So many thoughts fluttered her little mind but none caused her to question her actions. Her big eyes flooded with tears and pain surged through her little body as she laid tightly against Mr. Richard.

"My name is all I owe you." She managed between sobs as tears flowed from her eyes. She was not suppose to think of her mother or father who was killed in Iraq or her uncle's Jalal and Iqbal or her other relatives, but that's what motivated her.

Her small hand pressed the dull end of the blade and it's handle tightly against Mr. Richard's neck. The way she was taught in combat training, it took skill not to cut your opponents neck because it took all her might from not leaning forward so she had to speak quickly.

"My name is Tinsia Bint Sandi, you knew my family."

From the way Carlton Richard's eye lit up it confirmed he knew her name. "How could you forget?" She asked as she relaxed the muscles in her body and fell forward cutting Carlton Richards throat like a melon as she was trained.

Richard felt the blade slicing through his skin, no longer thinking he grabbed the blade, but to no avail the sharpness of the knife cut though his hand like butter. But better his hand then his neck. That was the shift he needed to push Tinsia's little body off of him.

She fell onto the floor then bounced up swinging the knife to keep the much larger man at bay, "You think this is over!" she turned screamed and ran to the door and pulled the door open. She didn't run out, instead she took a step outside the door and continued screaming only this time she started screaming hysterically, incoherently as if she was calling for help.

Richard kept his eyes on her as he recovered one of his fingers and something to rap his hand with. He opened his desk draw where he took out a handkerchief to rap his hand then reached back into his desk and removed a pearl handle chrome .357 colt.

At the sight of the gun Tinsia stop screaming and took a step back while keeping her eyes on Richard, "He's in there." she said pointing and out of nowhere tears poured from her eyes as she began to sob uncontrollably. Richard stopped in his tracks overwhelmed by the little girl's drastic change in behavior, and then he understood.

Carlton Richard's face was turning pale from the lost of blood but once he seen Agent Brinsky rush into his study Richard's face turned red instantly.

"Agent Black!" Agent Brinsky called out. "Agent Black come up here I found the girl." She yelled out a second time as she inched towards Mr. Richard with her gun raised on the ready.

"If you move I will kill." She warned. "Now drop your gun slowly." Brinsky said as she gestured for him to sit the gun on his desk. "Drop your gun!" She screamed.

"Gun?" Special Agent Black replied as he turned into the study and opened fire on Carlton Richard. Agent Black fired one shot then everyone stopped and looked at each other.

Brinsky looked at SAB, SAB kept his eye on Carlton Richard who stood there with his .357 still in his hand watching Tinsia as she walked into the room as calmly as she did the first time when he first seen her, only this time she didn't have that little girl's smile.

Blood squirted out of the hole in Carlton Richards head and he fell to the floor. Tinsia turned to Agent Brinsky "Thank you for saving my life, he kidnapped me from my home and held me here." Tinsia said calmly then looked at Agent Black. When she seen the people who were at the party standing in the door way she stared at them for a moment and shook her head.

"Didn't you'll hear me scream? Why didn't you'll help me?" Tinsia asked then ran out of the room. Tinsia made it down the long hallway that lead to the steps and paused, she had to do a double take. She didn't believe what she seen. She reached up and removed the frame from the wall. She then went and got into the car she came in and she waited.

"What you got there kid?" Sajud asked as he climbed into his car.

Tinsia looked up at Sajud with real tears in her eyes this time. "Look my father is in the picture." She said like the little girl she was.

Agent Black curiously took the frame from Tinsia and looked at the picture that had four people standing in front of the embassy in

Iraq. Dercole was standing behind Carlton Richard and Senator Borish. They were standing next to Tinsia's father and owner of Barakata Oil, Talib Abdul Rahman and his translator Mariam Sajud Black and they all were smiling into the camera.

That was the last picture taken of Tinsia's father Talib Abdul Rahman and his translator and the last time they were seen alive. This was the picture that said a thousand words.

Special Agent Black glanced over at Tinsia's face to see if this picture had as much meaning to her as it did to him. Her face was almost void of any feelings, but there was what looked like contentment as she returned his stare.

He also felt content in an odd kind of way, but that was not what put him at ease. By design he just killed an American, soon to be senator. As a reinstated federal agent there was a tinge of guilt.

For all intensive purposes they sent Cortex to Special Agent Black. Now, they sent Special Agent Black to Cortex and now he knew why, this picture spoke volumes.

The picture also brought a smile to Mr. Black Sr., seeing his wife's last smile. In seeing Dercole in the picture Mr. Black Sr., was even more content knowing he avenged his wife.

RECOMMENDED READING FOR ALL AGES, COLORS AND INTELLECT
FOUNDATION BUILDERS IN A BOOKSTORE NEAR YOU.
"THE TRUTH SHALL NOT ONLY SET YOU FREE, IT GIVES YOU POWER
OVER YOUR SURROUNDINGS!"

| | |
|---|---|
| Black Robes White Justice *by:* | *Bruce Wright* |
| Illusions of Justice *by:* | *Lenox Hinds (Iowa University)* |
| The Browder Files *by:* | *Anthony T. Browder* |
| Bad Blood *(The Tuskegee Experiment) by:* | *James H. Jones* |
| From Superman to Man *by:* | *J. A. Rogers* |
| Assata Shakur *by:* | *Assata Shakur* |
| Stolen Legacy *by:* | *George M.G. James* |
| Miseducation of the Negro *by:* | *Carter G. Woodson* |
| They Stole It but You Must Return It *by:* | *Richard Brown* |
| The Isis Papers *by:* | *Dr. Frances C. Wesling* |
| The Gnostic Gospels *by:* | *Elaine Pagels* |
| Possessing the Secrets of Joy *by:* | *Alice Walker* |
| The Conspiracy To Destroy Black Boys *by:* | *Jwanza Kujufi* |
| Before Columbus *by:* | *Ivan Van Sertima* |
| Christianity, Islam and the Negro Race *by:* | *Blyden* |
| Glory of The Black Race *by:* | *El Jahees* |
| 7 African Arabian Wonders of the World *by:* | *Khalid Mansour* |
| Blood In My Eye *by:* | *George Jackson* |
| The Autobiography of Malcolm X *by:* | *Alex Haley & Malcolm X* |
| The Holy Quran translated *by:* | *Yusuf Ali* |

## HOOD WARS by ESCO
**ISBN#** 978-0-9844071-4-9
Page count: **397** Price Book **$16.99**
Prison order price: **$11.00**

Nina and Toast are two disheartened enemies who vowed to "WARN AND PROTECT" each other over the course of an impending war. Eventually Nina feels betrayed, after a rush of slugs nearly claim her life. She goes on a manhunt tracking down Toast, revealing her own treacherous behavior to her inner circle. Unfortunately, her acts of desperation may soon get her killed!

Toast has too much to worry about than explaining his innocence to Nina. At the same time, he and his "FLUNKIES" are having a transformation of power. Toast must find ways to keep himself and his underlings safe from the most monstrous gang in the city. Plus the risk of death ten folds when Toast soldiers have a clash of ideas and a division of loyalty. Plunged into a world where HONOR and RESPECT is cut paper thin. Toast is not going to know who to trust.

Who will be left standing when the smoke clears at the end of this bloody tale of deception, betrayal and survival of the fittest? Will Nina be able to eliminate Toast before her own treacherous past catches up with her? Will toast find sanctuary away from the madness; or will he walk right into the line of fire set up by either friend or foe?

D.D. Ellis explosive novel HOOD WARS is non-stop action, filled with larger than life characters, and will keep you asking "What will happen next?"   It's a must read!!!

### *FIVE STAR REVIEW*
Esco you got one. HOOD WARS truly a great read.
Finally a representation of a writer from Allah Born.
Very entertaining! Keep pushing, we're moving......

GOAT
Albany, New York

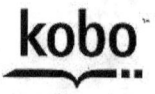

**FALLEN ANGEL** by FruitQuan
**ISBN#** 978-0-9844071-3-2
Page Count **333** Price Book **$15.99**
Prison order price: **$11.00**

From the Brownsville slums of Brooklyn, New York and Los Angeles, California all the way to the Federal Penitentiary, the hourglass is ticking, the streets are watching, and Gangstaz gotta KEEP IT GULLY!

With Albert Anastasia roots and links to the Biggie Smalls vs Tupac rival, Brooklyn's home of the legendary Mike Tyson is saturated with history...... Brownsville has a story to tell.

### *FIVE STAR REVIEW*

Fallen Angel is a story of the games that are played on the streets; some people's reality. The characters in the book remind me of actual people that live & hang in the streets of the five boroughs (NYC). I found myself constantly picking up the book to read at every opportunity that I could.

FruitQuan did an excellent job characterizing Hurricane, the main character as well as the others (Mama Maxie, Pale Face etc). Hurricane reminds me of "Midnight" from Sistah Souljah's book "A Coldest Winter Ever". The story is written whereas you know Hurricanes every thought, whether you agree with those thoughts or not. So if you like a book with lots of family love, street hustle, action & fast money this is the book for you."

Crystal
Brooklyn, NY

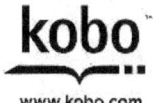

**WHAT'S NEXT** by Courtney B. Walker
Drama, Pain, Heartache & Betrayal
**ISBN#** 978-0-9844071-2-5
Page Count **249** Price Book **$12.99**
Prison order price: **$9.00**

The author weaves a dynamic plot showing how one young woman's life undergoes drastic changes with each situation she faces, much of which leads to more pain and heartbreak. The character, Angel Reneé Walker, is unlike other people in the world. She can tell what lies ahead, all the drama, pain, heartache, and betrayal. It all began on the first day of her senior year when her mother's life was taken in a car accident. Since then, her world has turned upside down.

Angel finds herself in difficult situations, while her relationship with her father is at its breaking point. It seems that nothing can go right. She starts to give up on life, on everything. When she meets someone who makes her believe there is still a chance, she feels hopeful again. But like everything else in her life, will this love be destroyed? Angel will be tested when a dark secret shocks her and she finds out that the one person she trusted most in the world was involved in the tragic accident that took her mother's life. Is she destined for a life of despair and betrayal? What's Next reveals all.

### *FIVE STAR REVIEW*

"I recently read "What's Next," and I was amazed. I thought that this book would be a self-help book to help young people deal with the trials of growing up. But I was wrong. It was real talk from the beginning to the end. The young Angel Reneé Walker goes through things that a lot of adults can't handle. She lives, learns and falls down. But most of all, she had to find a way out of the place where people hide to get away. I found that this book is inspirational and just what is needed in today's world for our young people, both guys and girls. Grief comes to us all, but not all of us make it through. The aspect I admire is how she maintains her social standing among her peers."

KAY JOHNSON
Brooklyn, NY

E-Books $7.99    www.kobo.com

**BROOKLYN ICE** by Anthony Brewer
**ISBN#** 978-0-9844071-0-1
Page Count **305** Price Book **$14.99**
Prison order price: **$11.00**

Brooklyn Ice follows its main character Theresa Jones. A Financial Consultant and Attorney; known through academic, corporate and judiciary realms as Ms. Jones. She is known on the streets and by friends as B.G. (short for Baby Girl), and there is only one thing she loves more than her desire to acquire money or her zeal for drama - and that's Joseph Cohen.

Joseph who is cut from the old school cloth of stick up kids use to rob banks, drug dealers and payrolls. He started investing money early on and sent his virgin love to school while he styled under the guise of a Real Estate Agent. That was back in the day, but now, the laid back, more reserved J.C. comes to find his Baby Girl has adopted his old gun slinging ways and combined them with her education and unrelenting Brooklyn ways.

Tempted by millions in diamonds, Joseph has decisions to make. In a time of recession, the Brooklyn bad boys are coming out with hopes Joseph will let Brooklyn do what it has always done - get money. Ride with J.C. or BG; she will not only get you money, but she'll show you how to use it. You decide. But whatever you do, don't get it twisted. The school girl is no longer taking lessons: she's giving them...... There's a new Brooklyn bully. Who would think it's a female?!

### *FIVE STAR REVIEW*

*"BROOKLYN ICE by Anthony Brewer is an exciting, breath-taking, fast pace novel to read. This book will have you on the edge of your seat waiting for the next piece of excitement. This book is definitely a page turner. BROOKLYN ICE is packed with plenty of action..."*

Barbara Morgan
ATL, Georgia

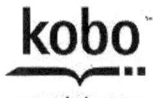

E-Books **$7.99**

**TERRORIST IN BROOKLYN** by Anthony Brewer
Revolutionary or Conspirator
**ISBN#** 978-0-9844071-1-8
Page Count **254** Price Book **$14.99**
Prison order price: **$11.00**

Terrorism activity has picked up on American soil as a result of the construction of an 80 billion dollar American oil project in Iraq, leaving the Federal Bureau of Investigation with work to do. With Corporate buildings getting blown up, dead bodies appearing out of thin air and the Bureau short on answers all fingers point to Special Agent Black of CTU.

No one ever thought terrorism would be on the door step of Brooklyn residents as victims or practitioners, but what is discover will change Brooklyn forever.

It doesn't help matters when Sheppard's Private Contracting Security Agency (Mercenaries) who served in the Iraq, Afghanistan and Saudi Arabia killing with impunity, have come to America after MOST WANTED terrorist that fled from Iraq seeking refuge in Brooklyn.

Equally alarming are the African American faces with international ties that are popping up as suspects of terrorism. In the midst of Agent Black's investigation, he connects Muslim residents from local Mosques supporting none terrorist. What's worse he finds he is not only a suspect, but a MOST WANTED.

With all eyes on Special Agent Black, he will have to choose between clearing his name when suspected of terrorism activity or making a name for himself by standing for justice against terrorist no matter who the perpetrators......

Charles H. Belim

E-Books $7.99   www.kobo.com

**SHOESHINE BOY** by Charles Belim
ISBN# **978-0-9844071-6-3**
Page count **269** Price Book **$14.99**
Prison order price: **$11.00**

The "Shoeshine Boy" saga chronicles events in the life of a young kid growing up in Boston, Massachusetts. At age ten he's given an opportunity to shine shoes in a shine parlor deep within the "Mob" controlled section of Boston's notorious 'North End'. Unbeknownst to him, the shine parlor is a front for illegal betting from horses to the local 'nigga number' in his community of Roxbury.

The experiences and exposure of that summer will catapult the Shoeshine Boy into being dubbed one of Boston's most infamous 'Common Known and Notorious Thieves.' The Shoeshine Boy story is about his beginning.

**"Payin' My Dues"**, **"Plastic Money"**, and **"Paper Money"** by the same author, will chronicle his rise, fall, and resurrection. Mr. Belim's resurrection as a new urban writer has given his readers a glimpse into the Black Underworld of trickery and deception.

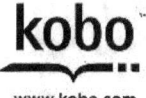

E-Books $9.99   www.kobo.com

**LOYALTY REIGNS by Japlin Cureton**
ISBN # **978-0-9844071-8-7**
Page Count **413** Price Book **$17.99**
Prison order price: **$11.00**

"Loyalty Reigns" exposes the raw and often ugly truth about survival in a world tainted by jealousy, rivalry, violence, drama and mayhem; disagreements settled only by bullets and blood. The question whose answer determines who lives or dies that day is, "Will Loyalty Reign or will the storms of betrayal make it hail?" Be for warned, it's not a fairy tale or a story for the squeamish or the faint-hearted, but if you're unafraid to be inoculated with a dose of reality, jump into a Destinations Cab and join Jap Cureton for an "adults-only" tour through the unforgiving world where only "Loyalty Reigns," and honor rules.

This story chronicles the act of deception where there is no honor amongst thieves; where mayhem thrives in a sinful world of MONEY, SEX, and POWER.   Decrypt coincidences, coordinated murders, set-ups, perpetrated by Blueberry, and dishonest Agents will test ones quest of LOYALTY REIGNS!

*Jap Cureton is presently at work on the second book of the "Loyalty Reigns" trilogy.*

E-Books $9.99   www.kobo.com

**INDICTED by Lamont Christian**
ISBN# **978-0-98440071-7-0**
Page Count **341** Price Book **$16.99**
Prison order price: **$11.00**

They say that there are two sides to every story and to every coin, but what most don't know is that there are two sides to a small section of the city's world Renown Island "MANHATTAN" and it all depends on which side you are on. Harlem always rung louder and there is only one thing that mattered above all and it's that "paper".

In this story of East meets west, the traditional fashion of how the sedative that is excreted from a syringe, through the eye of a needle and finally into the blood stream of heroin hungry veins, causes sides to clash. This eventually places the "self proclaimed king of Harlem" Lavell Collins in direct opposition with the eastside and that inadvertently puts Yvonne, Lavell's girlfriend in a freedom compromising, life altering situation.

INDICTED is a story that illustrates love, lost and the desperation that often justifies the behavior of those residing in Harlem and the various communities that mirror it. Places where addiction consumes the home, demoralizes the people and erodes the spirit. Like the many that came before it, INDICTED gives readers a unique and in depth look at a world where the social, economic mechanics, that has for generations plagued our culture, could be unfair and outright discriminative.

This goes beyond the 2014 version of Romeo & Juliet because it takes place in HARLEM where Lavell and Yvonne have to fight for everything, including the basic liberties such as life and love while fending for one another, even if it's by their own set of rules.

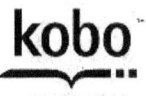

E-Books $10.99    www.kobo.com

**FANTASY BALL** by ADENA
ISBN#**978-0-9844071-9-4**
Page Count **448** Book Price **$17.99**
Prison order price: **$11.00**

ABANDONED 310 MILLION YEARS AGO, IN WHAT IS NOW SOUTHWESTERN PENNSYLVANIA, A GROUP OF BALLS ARE SLOWLY UNEARTHED DEEP IN A FAMILY COAL MINE. THE FIRST TO BE DISCOVERED IS A NINE FOOT TALL YELLOW FANTASY BALL. NEITHER, NASA OR OTHER SCIENTIST CAN IDENTIFY WHAT THE IMPENETRABLE SPHERE IS MADE OF.

WITH NO APPARENT USE OR VALUE, THE OWNER OF THE COAL MINE PLOPS THE BALL DOWN IN HIS BACK YARD FOR HIS 13 YEAR OLD SON TO PLAY ON. YET IT IS THE AUTISTIC NEIGHBOR GIRL WHO USES HER GIFT OF MENTAL TELEPATHY TO OPERATE THE YELLOW SPHERE. SO JOIN CHAD AND VENUS ON THEIR SOMETIMES DANGEROUS, YET ALWAYS THRILLING, ADVENTURES THROUGH TIME AND SPACE IN THE FANTASY BALL; THE FIRST BOOK IN THE SERIES.

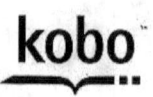

E-books $10.99   www.kobo.com

**JO ANN**
**"SHE ROSE FROM THE ASHES"**
ISBN # 978-0-9844071-5-6
Page Count: **376** Book Price: **$17.99**
Prison order price: **$11.00**

America, the most powerful country on earth, has produced some of the most prolific families on earth. One such family is the Douglass'. Spawned from England and hardened by the Civil War, the family history is intriguing (mixed heritage) ruthless, and unique. This story entails the first of the mixed heritage, Jo Ann Douglass, and the family members that blazed a burning trail through the civil war era and reconstruction. A taut, suspense filled story in which the protagonist joins the union army passing as a white man, and shares adventures with us as a war hero, feminist, Romantic Heroine, and business woman that happens to become the first black female woman of wealth, all the while harboring a viscous secret.

Travel with me down the pulse pounding, page turning road with
**"Jo Ann."**

Little known fact; over 250 women enlisted and fought in the civil war for both the Union and Confederacy as men, now comes the story of the only black women to do so!

# ORDER FORM

Name:_____

Address:_____

State:_____

Phone# _____

**Title(s) purchased:**

_____

_____    Ship: $2.50

_____    Total $_____

**Send Mail :**

New Era Books

1211 Atlantic Ave, Suite 303

Brooklyn, New York 11216

Purchase on line: www.newerabooks.net   or call 347-651-6366

Always include alternative book selection for unavailable books

Book Submissions & Inquiries: newerapublication@aol.com

Free shipping with the purchase of any two books.

## PRISON DIRECT

**Prison Direct:** Family and friends can send New Era books, posters, greeting cards directly to any inmate in State/Federal prison. New Era Books promotes education for this reason we sell books to the prison population at a discounted price. Order Prison Direct through newerabooks.com

### Rehabilitation Begins With Education......

www.ingramcontent.com/pod-product-compliance
Lightning Source LLC
Chambersburg PA
CBHW070900250626
47159CB00003B/1136